# The August Havens Chronicles

# Wanted

## Shelby Haisley

To Donna:
I hope you enjoy Wanted!
- Shelby Haisley

ISBN: 1494861011
ISBN-13: 978-1494861018

LCCN: 2014900978
CreateSpace Independent Publishing Platform
Charleston, SC

For Mom and Dad for supporting my writing career,
even when it seemed like too much of a struggle.
Thanks to Katelyn for being a wonderful friend and creating a
beautiful cover, too.
I love you all.

-S.E.H.

unnatural position. I knew she was already dead. "Oh, no," I sobbed. "Oh gosh, no. Don't do this to me. I don't want to die."

Dad took my hand. I tried not to notice that his hand was sticky with blood. "August, listen to me," he said calmly.

"Daddy, what happened? Don't leave me," I begged. "Don't leave me."

"Listen to me, sweetheart. This was not an accident, understand?"

My heart sank. "What? What do you mean?"

"August, this was a setup. You need to get out of here. You need to run as far and as fast as you can. There's a bag in the trunk. Grab it and run. Don't stop. Don't look back, no matter what happens. They will be looking for you, okay? So you just run."

"Who are 'they?'" I asked. "Who will be looking for me?" I was really confused and the fact that I had whiplash wasn't helping. "I'm not leaving you," I said. My father pulled a gun out of his jacket and pointed it in my direction. "Daddy?" I gasped fearfully.

He looked very determined. "Yes, you are. If they find out you exist, they will never let you go. Now go, August! Run!" He was breathing heavily now. "Go!"

I pushed against my door and managed to get it open. I stumbled on my burning ankle and fell to the pavement. "What's going to happen to you?" I cried.

"Don't worry about me. Just get out of here!"

"I can't do this."

"Yes, you can. Be strong, August. You still have a lot of strength left in you."

I nodded with tears streaming down my face. I pulled the trunk open, grabbed the black duffel bag inside, and ran down the Philadelphia streets. I didn't know where I was going, but I was getting away from the accident. *Why did this happen? Dad said that it wasn't an accident. Why wouldn't it be an accident?*

I was only a few blocks away when I was forced to stop since my ankle was killing me. I slid into an alley and sat on someone's back step. I put my head in my hands. "What am I going to do?" I sobbed. "My parents are dead, I'm all alone. What is going to happen to me?"

I sniffled and glanced at the bag. Something told me that it was important. I unzipped it and gasped when I pulled out a Smith & Wesson pistol. I dropped the gun in horror. "What the heck?" I wondered. I reached inside the bag and brought out a blue United States passport. I opened it and saw my photo, but a different name. "Madison Taylor Clark," I read.

I was shocked. Why had my father packed a bag for me with a gun and a fake passport? I rummaged through the bag some more and found hair dye, colored contacts, a couple changes of clothes, a cell phone, and a large envelope filled with money. A lot of money. My eyes grew wide as I flipped through the bills. "What is going on?" I whispered.

All of a sudden, light flooded the alley. I turned towards the light fearfully. I saw black silhouettes getting out of an SUV. My heart began to pound. I grabbed the bag and ran into the shadows.

"Stop, August!" a voice called. "We're with the police! We're not here to hurt you!"

I didn't listen. I just kept sprinting down the alleyway. *Dad must have a reason for me to escape the wreck. It was his dying wish for me to run. He had a bag packed full of things for me to start a new life under a different name.*

Just then, I ran smack-dab into a wire fence. I cried out as I fell back onto the concrete. Everything started to become very dizzy and I couldn't breathe. I couldn't find my bag; I must have thrown it. Hands grabbed my wrists and ankles. I shrieked when they touched my bad one. "Let go of me!" I cried. "Let me go!" I continued screaming as the two people carried me out of the alley. Then I felt a needle enter my skin and my world went dark.

~\*O\*~

I awoke and found myself lying in a hospital bed. Tubes snaked out of my arms and my ankle was wrapped in an ACE bandage. *What happened?* My head was throbbing and all I wanted to do was sleep. I then realized that someone was holding my hand. I focused on the person and sighed when I figured out who it was. "Jules?" I asked groggily. "Is that you?"

My cousin Juliet Spencer raised her head. "August?" she managed to choke. I could see tears in her eyes. She brushed her blond hair out of her face. "Are you okay? Are you in any pain?"

"Where am I?" I replied. "What happened?" I couldn't remember anything.

"You were in an accident earlier tonight, August," Jules said slowly, "do you remember?"

I shook my head. I couldn't recall any accident. Only my injuries made me believe that I could have been in one. I then noticed Jules' sister Natalie standing in the corner with tears streaming down her face. "Did something bad happen?" I implored. "Why are you guys crying?"

Jules couldn't look at me. "Tell me what happened," I ordered. Natalie started sobbing in the corner. Jules gave her a look.

"Stop it," she said softly. Natalie wiped her eyes.

I turned to Jules. "Jules?" I asked.

She sighed. "August, your parents were killed in the accident. They didn't make it."

I was horrified. "No," I whispered. "No, you're lying! You have to be lying! My parents are not dead!"

"Auggie, I'm so sorry, but they're gone."

"Where are they? I want to see them." I tried to get out of bed, but I was too weak. Jules laid me back down.

"Just remember them as they were. You need to rest."

"What's going to happen to me?" I gasped. "I have no one."

"You have me and Natalie," Jules said firmly. "We're not going to let anything happen to you." She tucked in my sheets.

"Now you rest," she commanded. "Nat and I have to talk to some people and figure out what we're going to do with you. Your parents' will has been found and that tells who your guardian is."

"It's you," I sniffed. "Dad told me that he and Mom put you down for my guardian."

"Well, we have to make it legal," she replied. "So we'll be right back. Call me on my cell if you need anything. Your cell phone is on the table." She gestured to the table next to my bed. "Love you." She kissed me on my forehead and left with Nat.

Still crying, I leaned back against my pillows. *My parents are dead. I'm all alone. Why can't I remember anything? Something traumatic must have happened for me to forget.*

The door opened and a tall African-American woman walked in. She sat in the chair next to me. "Hello, August," she said.

"Who...who are you?" I asked.

"My name is Celia Keene. I'm a...old friend of your father's. I'm so sorry about their passing."

"Why are you here?" I replied warily.

"I'm an investigator with the police. I just need to ask a few questions about the accident."

"I don't remember it," I said coldly. "I just found out that my parents are dead. Could you please leave me alone?"

"I'm afraid these questions can't wait. Now you were found in an alley three blocks from the accident site. You were so terrified, the EMT's had to sedate you in order to get you to the hospital. Can you tell me why you were that far away?"

"No," I answered. "I don't remember."

"What's the last thing you do remember?"

"Um..." I racked my brain. "My parents and I went to a movie. We got in the car together. That's all I know."

"Okay..." Celia wrote something down on a clipboard. "Do you know what caused the accident?"

"No. Ms. Keene, I told you that I don't remember the accident. I really don't. Could you please leave me alone? Maybe if I think for a while, I'll remember something."

Celia gave a small smile, but I could tell she was frustrated. "Of course, August. I'll come back in a little bit." She stood up and left the room, almost running into Jules.

"Who are you?" Jules implored. "What were you doing in there? Don't you know that she is traumatized?" Celia was already gone.

"Who was that?" she asked. I shrugged my shoulders.

"I don't know. She claimed to be an investigator with the police."

Jules scoffed. "I wouldn't be surprised if she was a reporter. Yell if she comes in here again, okay? I don't want her talking to you. I'm going to go tell the nurse not to let her in." My cousin left and I was left alone. I looked out my window at the city. The lights were beautiful late at night. Dad and I used to go up on the roof of our house and look at them every night. Now, he was gone. I started to cry again.

The door flew open and Celia came in followed by two strong-looking men. I backed up instinctively. "Now will you be willing to talk to me, August?" she said coldly.

"What do you want?" I cried. "I don't know anything!"

"I don't believe you. You knew enough to run from the accident. We found a bag in the alley with certain paraphernalia in it. You know something, August. That's why the CIA wants you."

"The CIA? What?"

"You're coming with me. Don't fight me or I will hurt you. Understand?"

I could only nod. My throat had gone dry and I couldn't scream. A flash of memory went through my head. *Be strong, August. You still have a lot of strength left in you.*

"Dad," I whispered.

"What did you say?" Celia asked.

I smiled. "I'm not going with you," I replied. "You'll have to kill me first." Using what strength I had, I pulled out the tubes in my arms and ran out of the hospital room. I ran past Jules, who was still speaking with the nurse.

"August!" she cried. "What are you doing?"

"Stop that girl!" Celia yelled. "She's an escaped fugitive!"

*What? A fugitive?* I knew that now I had to run. I couldn't remember the accident, but apparently I had known enough to get away. The CIA wanted me, but I didn't know why. *Maybe I knew something that I couldn't remember.*

I turned a corner and ran past a storage closet. Someone grabbed my wrist and yanked me inside. I opened my mouth to scream, but a strong hand covered it. "Shh, August. I'm a friend of your Dad's," a male voice said.

I struggled even more. I managed to get the man's hand off my mouth. "Yeah, right! That's what the woman said, and now she's trying to kill me!"

"Celia?" the man said in surprise. "She's here?"

"Please, just let me go," I begged. "I haven't seen you. I just need to get out of here."

"And go where, August? Home? There are ten CIA agents searching it now. Your picture is plastered all over the news. The airports and the bus stations already have your photo. You're a sitting duck."

"Who are you?" I hissed, attempting to see his face. The room was too dark, though.

"My name is Aaron Steele. I knew your dad. We used to work together when you were a little girl."

"How do I know that I can trust you? For all I know, you could be planning to kill me or turn me over to Celia."

Aaron sighed. "Your name is August Marie Havens, your parents were Conner and Lily Havens, and you were born in August. What else do you want to know?"

"That's not specific enough."

"Look August, I don't want to be here. The only reason that I'm standing here is because I made a promise to your father that I would keep an eye on you if anything happened to him. And since he's dead, I'm here."

"How are we going to get out of here?"

"Leave that to me." He opened the door a crack. "Stay here."

I nodded. Aaron leaned out of the closet. "Come with me."

I followed him into the hallway. I then saw my new ally's face for the first time. He was shorter than I expected, only a few inches taller than me. He had longish brown hair and cold brown eyes that cut into whatever he turned his gaze on. He was handsome, I had to admit. Way too old for me, though.

We didn't speak as we snuck through the halls of the hospital. I was too scared to talk and Aaron didn't seem like the type to converse. It almost seemed like we were home free until a voice cut the silence.

"August?" It was Jules. I turned around in shock. She was standing right behind me along with Celia. "What are you doing?"

Without even blinking, Aaron snatched Jules and put a gun to her head. I screamed and backed away from him.

Celia drew a gun and pointed it at Aaron's chest. "Stop right there, Steele," she commanded.

"Not going to happen, Celia. Besides, she isn't even important. It's August you want." He pushed Jules away and grabbed me. I gasped as I felt cold steel against my temple. "You can't shoot me without hitting her. I know she's valuable. Losing her would mean losing the final piece." He was walking backwards down the hallway towards the front door. I was struggling to get away, but curious as to what Aaron was talking about.

Celia and her men remained still. "And what are you going to do with her, Aaron? Auction her off to the highest bidder?"

"No," Aaron answered. "I'm going to keep a promise." With that, he scooped me up and ran towards the front doors.

"Where are we going?" I cried.

"Away from here," he replied. He thrust the doors open and ran into the parking lot. I clung to him to keep myself from falling. Aaron rushed to a sedan and threw me into the backseat. I landed with a thump that jostled my injured ankle. I bit my lip to prevent a scream.

Aaron jumped into the driver's seat and turned the key. Just as he was about to back up, something hit the car. I leaned out the window and saw Jules. "Let August go!" she shrieked.

"Jules?" I said in surprise.

"Seriously?" Aaron opened his door and yanked Jules inside the car, throwing her into the passenger seat. Then he slammed his foot on the gas and we took off into the night.

"Where are we going?" Jules asked, repeating my question from earlier. "This is kidnapping!"

"Yes, you're very right about that," Aaron admitted. "But you would probably like to be with me over Celia."

"Who are you?" Jules accused angrily. "Some crazy lunatic looking for a good time?"

"No," he reassured. "I'm a friend of Conner's. I'm here to protect August. And now you, I guess. Trust me, you're better off here in this car than with Celia right now."

"That still doesn't explain tossing me in this car against my will."

"It was either that or running you over."

I watched the two of them banter back and forth. I found it entertaining actually, even though we were fleeing from the government who wanted me for some odd reason. *Aaron called me "the final piece." The final piece to what? I'm nothing special. I'm just a recently orphaned teenage girl.*

"You still haven't told me where you're taking us," Jules said crossly.

"For now, New York," Aaron answered. "I have some unfinished business there. From there, Europe. August, your father left a package for you in a bank in Zurich. He told me that you were only to open it upon his and your mother's deaths. He never said what was inside, but I'm guessing it was important."

"How...how did you know my father?" I questioned.

"We used to be partners. I always had his back and he had mine. At one point, I think he and your mother were going to name me to be your guardian. I'm glad that Juliet got picked instead," he said with a laugh.

10

"Do you work with the CIA?" Jules wondered.

"Yes," Aaron replied quietly. "I have for the past fifteen years. But not anymore. Celia will tell you that I 'went rogue.' I just decided that I was done killing people. Plus, I need to take care of some things."

"I hope you know that I am not going along with this willingly," Jules put in firmly. "The only reason I haven't tried to escape this car is because I know that we have no chance on our own."

"That's right. On your own, the chances of you two surviving are slim to none. As long as August is alive, they will never stop searching for her."

"What is so special about me?" I implored.

Aaron went silent. "I promised that I wouldn't tell you. Everything you want to know is in that safe-deposit box." He refused to say anything more. "Why don't you both go to sleep?" he suggested. "It's going to be a long drive."

I leaned back against my seat and closed my eyes. As I did, another flash of memory appeared. *Listen to me, sweetheart. This was not an accident, understand?*

My eyes snapped open. "Oh Daddy, what were you and Mom into?" I whispered.

# 2

I looked out the window of the car at the city lights. We had been driving through Philadelphia for a while in an attempt to find a way out without being caught by local police. Silence filled the car since none of us knew what to say.

I sighed and tried to figure out why I couldn't remember the accident. Why had I been found three blocks away from the scene? Why would I ever leave my parents behind?

"Deep in thought?" Aaron asked.

I nodded. "Why can't I remember probably the most important event in my life?"

"Shock, probably," he replied. "Or you might have been injured."

"I have a lump on my forehead," I said while feeling it.

"That might be it," he answered. "I know you'll figure it out."

"I just wish I knew something," I wondered. "I'm sick over it. My parents are killed and I can't remember anything. All I know is that I ran away and woke up in a hospital. Why would I leave them alone to suffer? It makes my stomach turn." I realized that tears were streaming down my face. I wiped them away angrily. I wasn't going to show my weakness to him.

Aaron had already seen my tears, though. "It's okay to cry. You have just lost your parents. Besides, it's good to let out your emotions. It reminds you that you can still feel."

I leaned back into my seat. "So you were in the CIA?" I asked.

"Yeah, for fifteen years. I was recruited while in the Marines."

"What did you do?"

He sighed. "Honestly, I killed people. Men, women, even children. I never was given a reason on some of them. I was told that I was fighting for my country, but I'm not so sure of that anymore. You would have been doing the same thing if Celia had gotten her hands on you."

"What do they want with me? I know you have an idea."

"You'll find out in Zurich." That was all he would say on the subject.

By this time, we had come up to a roadblock. Aaron became rigid. "August, there's a bag of clothing under my seat. Put on something that fits and act natural. Juliet, remain calm. If you panic, the officers will know it's us." He began feeding her a cover story while I threw on a pair of jeans and a sweatshirt over my hospital gown. I handed a denim jacket up to Jules for her to use. My heart was pounding. I couldn't get caught. Not now. I had to know why my parents were dead and why I was in danger. I pulled my hood over my head and quietly turned my face away from the window so the officer wouldn't see my bruised face .

Aaron drove the car to the roadblock. The police officer shone his flashlight into our vehicle. "Sorry folks, we just need to check the trunk and you can be on your way." Aaron obligingly popped the trunk and an officer went to check it. My breathing began to become heavy. I bit my lip in an attempt to remain calm. Jules was sitting up straight in her seat.

"What is this about?" she asked stiffly.

"Just a couple of fugitives who escaped federal custody," the police officer replied. "There's nothing to worry about, ma'am. They'll be caught soon."

Jules nodded. "Of course."

I couldn't believe how easily she was lying. Usually Jules was a horrible liar. *Well desperate times call for desperate measures, I guess.* I saw the other officer shake his head and slam the trunk shut.

"You're free to go," the main officer told Aaron. Aaron gave him a smile and we began to slowly drive away.

"That was close," I said while trying to slow my heart rate.

Aaron laughed. "Not really. Just wait until we get to the airport."

"I don't think I want to know," Jules put in. "It sounds dangerous."

"Don't worry, Jules," I replied. "Just go with the flow."

"If that's the plan, I'm not putting much confidence in it."

I sighed and just shut my mouth. I knew that Jules didn't want to be here, but there was nothing I could do about it. I had to know what happened to my parents, even if I had to listen to my cousin complain about how much danger we were in now.

"We're low on gas," Aaron stated. "I'll have to stop soon."

I noticed a strange look on Jules' face. *What are you thinking about?* I wondered. I didn't have time to ponder this since Aaron had pulled into a gas station in a small town. He got out of the car and went to pump gas.

"Is it all right if August and I go use the bathroom?" Jules asked innocently. "It will be a long drive if we don't stop again."

Aaron just waved his hand in consent. Jules practically dragged me out of the car and towards the station. "Hey, take it easy," I hissed. "My ankle is still killing me."

"Sorry," she whispered. "But this might be our only chance."

"Our only chance to do what?" I was feeling uneasy as I saw the same strange look cloud my cousin's face.

"Run," Jules breathed. Then, in the blink of an eye, she grabbed me by the wrist and yanked me down the darkened streets.

"Jules!" I cried. "What are you doing?"

"I'm saving you, August. Aaron is crazy. He already held us hostage. He's probably planning to kill us in a matter of time. We have to get away from him."

"No, we can't!" I yelled. "Aaron is my only lead! I need to find out what happened to my parents! If I lose him, I lose everything. Plus, we are wanted, Jules. If we're caught, they *will* kill us. Don't you understand?"

"August, I have friends in Philly. They can hide us until this whole mess is straightened out. Then we can go back to our normal lives. Your parents were killed in an *accident*, Auggie. There's no conspiracy surrounding it. It was a horrible and freak accident. A drunk driver slammed into your car and killed your parents. Right now he is sobering up in jail and soon he will be put on trial. That is who you should be focusing on, Auggie. Focus on putting that miserable, murderous drunk in jail for the rest of his life!"

I realized I was crying again. "Jules, I believe Aaron when he says he knew my dad. He knows what happened to my parents. I just have to trust him to help me find the answers."

"August, I can't let you do that. I'm your legal guardian and I have to do what's best for you. Please, just come with me. Don't make me force you."

I slowly began to back away from my cousin. "Jules, I have to go with him. Even if I go to jail forever, I will do it if it means I can find out about my parents. Go back to Philly and stay with your friends. Maybe the CIA will clear your name soon."

"Don't, Auggie." I saw her walking towards me.

"I'm sorry, Jules." I ran towards the end of the alley that we were in and towards the gas station where Aaron was. I was shocked when I didn't see his car.

"See?" Jules spat. "He doesn't care about you. You were only a distraction so he could get out of the hospital!"

"No..." I whispered. "That can't be true. He wanted to help

me."

"Come on, August. Let's just go back." She started to lead me away.

All of a sudden, a black SUV came barreling on top of us. We jumped out of its way. The vehicle stopped and two men got out and headed towards us. "Jules, run," I said through gritted teeth. My cousin was frozen and one of the men grabbed her. He pulled her inside the SUV without a word.

*"August!"* Jules screamed.

"No!" I shrieked. The SUV took off with my helpless cousin inside. I was about to run after them, but a hand slipped over my mouth and dragged me into the alley. I kicked and screamed, but my captor was too strong.

"Calm down, August! It's just me!"

I gasped. "Aaron? You didn't leave?"

"No, I didn't leave! I saw those agents and I knew I needed to get out of there before they recognized me. I was just looking for you and Juliet."

"They took Jules!" I cried. "They took her!"

"I know," Aaron replied.

"Well we just can't stand here! We have to do something!"

"It's too late, August." I saw that we were standing in front of a blue car. "I'm sorry that I have to do this, but you can't keep running." He picked me up and deposited me in the back seat. Then he handcuffed my wrist and put the other on the handle on the inside of the door. I cringed when I heard the locks click shut.

"You're crazy!" I screamed. "You can't keep me locked up like a prisoner!"

"Unfortunately, I can." He shut the door and climbed into the front seat. He drove off in the opposite direction of the SUV.

"You have to turn around," I begged. "We can't just leave her!"

"Juliet is a strong woman," Aaron said. "She'll be all right."

"No, she won't!" I disagreed. "They're going to torture her

and it's all my fault for dragging her into this!"

"Do you know how stupid it was to run off, August? You could have been captured too, and carted back to Celia. You are who she wants. Juliet is just bait. If you go after her, you'll be caught. I cannot and will not let that happen. I am your only chance of survival, understand?"

I was slowly formulating a plan in my mind. "I understand." I cautiously phrased my next words. "Aaron, if you want me to trust you, and my full cooperation, then you'll take off these handcuffs so I won't feel like my life is in jeopardy, okay?" I was hoping that he would take pity on me.

Aaron looked back at me before fumbling around in his coat pocket. "Here," he said while giving me a little silver key. I grabbed it and unfastened my wrist from the cuff. Then, I quickly pulled up the lock and opened the door. I was bailing!

"Hey! Not cool!" Aaron yelled as he grabbed my ankle to prevent me from escaping. Somehow, he pulled me in, shut my door, reattached the handcuff, and managed to keep driving. I was proud of myself for giving him a good kick in the face in the process. I gave him a death glare as we drove along.

"I'll scream," I threatened. "I can still roll down the window."

"Good thing the windows are childproofed, then," Aaron replied. "August, you have to trust me. I have been chasing after you for twelve hours straight. If I hadn't grabbed you back there, those agents would have killed Juliet and taken you back to Langley. Now, they have leverage. They will keep Juliet alive as long as you're free. But once you turn yourself in, they will kill her. Do you understand?"

I was understandably terrified. I was just now realizing how much danger I was really in. But that didn't stop me from wanting to free Jules. "We have to save Jules before it is too late," I pleaded. "She won't survive with them. Please, Aaron. We can turn the car around and save her. She's the only family I have left. I can't lose her."

Aaron didn't answer. Instead, he focused on driving. My

blood began to boil. I couldn't believe  he wasn't listening to me. "Hey!" I yelled. "I am not leaving my cousin for dead!" He didn't say a word. I angrily kicked his seat and swore. "Do you not have a soul?" I accused. "How can you let an innocent person suffer?" I felt tears rolling down my cheeks again.

"August, this is for your own good," I heard him say through gritted teeth.

"Handcuffing me to a car door is for my own good? Kidnapping me and holding a gun to my head is for my own good? You're crazy!" I cried.

"First off, the safety was on the whole time. Second, I did those things to protect you. Your life depends on me."

"What about handcuffing me? Is that to protect me, too?" I gave him a wry smile. I was ticked off that he was technically holding me against my will and that he was refusing to help Jules, but at least he cared about me.

"Well, yes. That is to keep you from running away again. You have to believe you are in danger, August. The CIA wants you for some sick, twisted reason. Your parents' bodies were still warm when Celia went after you. She is not wasting time and she will not stop until she has you in her custody. It is up to me to keep you alive and safe for the time being. I don't have to be here, August. I have problems of my own and I dropped everything to come after you. I could easily go back to my old life but I promised your father I would keep an eye on you and I will. It doesn't mean that I'm going to like it."

"Why would my father choose you?" I asked. "I've never even heard of you before."

"Your father and I were best friends when we were working together. He trusted that I could protect you if anything happened to him and your mother."

"So...he knew that he was in danger?"

"You could say that. I can't tell you anything else, August. You'll have to hear the rest from him when you open the safe deposit box."

I sighed. I really wished that Aaron wasn't so evasive about my parents. I needed to know the truth and what happened to them, especially since I couldn't even remember the accident that killed them. I looked at the clock. 3 AM. My parents had only been dead for ten hours. In those ten hours, I had transformed from a normal teenage girl into a broken, tired, and orphaned fugitive. I had met a man who I still was wary about trusting him with my life, and I was now on the run from the government. I still didn't know why they wanted me and I wasn't sure if I would ever know. I had lost my cousin to the government and I had no idea if she was even still alive. *"August!"* I could still hear her shriek. I grimaced at the memory.

"Are you okay?" Aaron asked. "Are any of your injuries hurting you?"

"No," I answered. "I'm just thinking about Jules and my parents."

"Don't worry about Juliet," he said reassuringly. "They won't hurt her. She's just going to be bait in order to get you to come to them." He paused for a moment. "Do you remember anything about the accident? Any little bit can help a lot."

I bit my lip. "I remember two things my dad said to me. 'Be strong, August. You still have a lot of strength in you.' He also said, 'Listen to me, sweetheart. This was not an accident, understand?' I know it's not much, but it's all I can remember."

"It's totally fine. You'll recall more soon. I know you will figure it out."

I nodded. "I know. It's just frustrating. Almost like a jigsaw puzzle that you can't figure out, you know?"

"You will find the answers you're looking for in Zurich, I promise." All of a sudden, he went silent and leaned towards the radio. His eyes grew wide. "Listen," he ordered.

*"A fatal car accident claimed two lives last evening in Philadelphia. At approximately five o'clock, Donald McBride drove through a red light while severely intoxicated and struck a car containing Conner, Lily, and their teenage daughter August Havens. Conner and Lily were pronounced dead at the scene while August was taken to a nearby hospital. She is still in a coma as of this time. Mr. McBride is currently being held in police custody*

*and is expected to be transferred to the state prison later today. A trial date has not been confirmed yet. Services for the two victims will be held on June 22."*

"They lied," I said in shock. "Why?"

"If they proclaim you a fugitive, it will only cause confusion in the media. Most likely, they will lie by keeping you in the "coma" and kill you when deemed necessary. It's an easier way to tidy up the mess they have created. Plus, if they do catch you, if you're already considered dead, no one will be looking for you."

I felt my heart begin to pound. I thought of my cousin Natalie and her fiancé James. I had no idea what they knew. They had to be worried sick about Jules and me. I envisioned them, scared out of their minds and waiting in a waiting room. I then remembered my best friend Blaire Pruitt. She had to be scared, too. *I can never go back to that life. I will never be able to reassure them I'm okay.* The thought made me want to cry again. *No. You have to be brave. You have to figure out why the CIA wants you and why your parents were killed.*

"What are we going to do, Aaron?" I asked. "It seems like you're the only person I can trust right now."

"I have to stop in New York for a couple of days, but then we'll head to Zurich to get that safe deposit box your father left you. I promise that you'll find all of the answers you're looking for there."

I nodded. "I hope you're right."

"Why don't you try to get some rest? I'll wake you up when we get there."

"Okay." I quietly leaned my head against my seat and closed my eyes. This time, there were no memories of my parents haunting my dreams. *Please let me remember something soon.* I begged. *I need to know the truth.*

# 3

Agent John Regan stood rigidly inside Director Celia Keene's office. "How could you have messed up this much?" Celia asked coldly. "I asked you to bring August Havens, not Juliet Spencer!"

"There were two blond women on the side of the road," Regan tried to explain. "I just grabbed the one closest to the car. It was only when we drove off that I realized my mistake. By the time we turned around, the girl was gone."

"Did you think about maybe checking the two women more thoroughly before driving off?" Celia was livid. "August is the final piece to Operation Lark, Regan. If we lose her, we lose everything!"

Regan was trembling. He knew it was only a matter of time until Celia made him pay for bringing the wrong girl. "What if we use Juliet as bait?" he suggested meekly. "August may try to save her."

"Interrogate her for now, Regan," Celia replied tiredly. "I'll decide what we'll do with Juliet later. Find out where Steele has taken August. And try not to screw up this time," she added angrily.

He nodded and hurried out of the office. Once he was in the hallway, he realized that the other agents around him were staring. He straightened his tie with shaky hands. "Carry on," he said in a tone that attempted to sound authoritative. The others simply shook their heads and tried to hide smiles and laughs behind files and clipboards. Regan only scoffed and marched down the hall towards the room where Juliet Spencer was being held. *Be prepared to tell me all you know, Juliet.*

~*O*~

Jules woke up to cramps in her arms. She slowly opened her eyes and attempted to move her arms to get the blood flowing again. She was shocked when she realized that her wrists were handcuffed behind her back. "Hello?" she called hoarsely. Her throat was extremely dry. *How long have I been asleep?* "Where am I?"

"You're in a secret location, Miss Spencer." A man with brown hair and sharp blue eyes walked out of the shadows. He wore a black suit and tie and looked very clean cut. It was the look in his eye that made her feel uneasy. He seemed very frustrated and a little frightening.

"Who are you?" Jules demanded.

"My name is Agent John Regan. I work for the FBI. I just want to ask you a few questions about your cousin's whereabouts." His voice sounded calm, which made Jules relax a little.

"Why do you want to know about August?" she asked.

"I'm afraid your cousin has been mixed up in a small problem. You know about Aaron Steele, correct?"

"He kidnapped August and me," Jules replied with contempt.

"That's right, Juliet. He did. We just want to get August back, okay? We want her to be brought back safely. It would help us if you would tell me where Aaron and August were going."

"I...I don't know," Jules answered vaguely. She still felt like there was something off about this man. "Aaron never told me.

He seemed more concerned about August anyway."

Agent Regan's expression changed to one unreadable. "I don't believe you, Juliet. Steele would have told you something."

"He didn't. I wasn't with him that long. I was actually trying to get away from him when you guys picked me up." She realized with fear that he did not want to keep August safe. "Can you please take off the handcuffs? My wrists are hurting."

"I'm afraid I can't, Juliet. You are under suspicion as well."

"Of what?" Jules asked in horror. "I haven't done anything wrong!"

"You aided and abetted two fugitives. You did try to get away, which we appreciate. But it is still on you. If you tell me where August is, We will lift the charge."

"Why are you so concerned with August? Why does the CIA want her?" she cried.

"We can't say. You don't have clearance."

"I won't tell you where she is unless I know why you want her so badly," Jules said firmly. "You won't get anything out of me, Regan."

Regan smiled slowly. "That's where you're wrong, Juliet. I can get anything out of you with the proper leverage. I'll be back shortly. Maybe you'll feel up to chatting then." He opened the door and walked out of the room.

"I'll never tell you where she is!" Jules screamed as the door slammed. "Never!" She hung her head and started to cry. *How did I get stuck in this nightmare?* She knew she had done the right thing. Something was wrong about this whole situation. *They referred to August as a fugitive.* Her heart began to beat faster. *They don't want to help her. They want to capture her.* How had her cousin been caught up in this mess? "Please stay safe, August," she whispered. "I won't forgive myself if you end up dying because of me."

~*O*~

I awoke with a start. I couldn't remember the nightmare that

I had just woken up from, but it was horrible. For a second, I didn't know where I was. "Mom? Dad?" I said softly. Then, I recalled the night before. The awful accident, the escape in the middle of the night, and Jules' capture. The pain in my chest came back in full force as I remembered that I was an orphan.

Aaron looked at me in the rearview mirror. I saw pity in his eyes. "Are you all right?"

I managed to nod. "I think so. Just a bad dream."

"Do you want to talk?"

"Not right now," I answered. "It still hurts."

"Okay." He seemed to understand that I needed space. "We're pretty close to the city," he said in an attempt to change the subject.

"That's good," I said halfheartedly. I still didn't know why we were going to New York, but I trusted Aaron and knew it had to be for a good reason. I was frustrated that we weren't going straight to Switzerland to open my father's box. *Be patient. Aaron has his reasons.* I watched the skyline of the city become closer and closer. I rubbed my eyes in an attempt to get the sleep out of them. I felt the puffiness from crying and winced. *Why me? Why target my family?* "I expect answers from you once we reach Europe," I told Aaron. "I can't just sit here and wonder why I have a target painted on my back."

"I will tell you what I can, August. We just have to pick up something here."

The car wound through the tight streets packed with vehicles. We had not managed to skip the morning rush hour and were therefore stuck in traffic. I sighed as I watched the sun rise over the city. "What are we picking up?" I asked.

"An old friend," Aaron answered cryptically.

About an hour later, we drove up an alleyway and Aaron parked the car. "Come on, we can't be seen here for long." He unlocked my handcuff and helped me out of the car. I bit back a cry of pain when I stood on my injured ankle. Aaron saw the look on my face, though. "We need to get that fixed," he stated with concern.

"I don't even know what happened," I replied. "I'm guessing that I hurt it in the accident, but I don't know if it is broken or sprained."

Aaron nodded and helped me walk towards an apartment building. It was built of stone and was five stories tall. It looked nice enough, definitely not a slum. I limped up the steps to the front door. Aaron secretly pushed the buzzer for an apartment. I couldn't read the name since he was blocking the speaker.

*"Confirm identity,"* a tinny voice commanded.

"Metal warrior," Aaron replied impatiently. "Let me in, Jase."

*"Identity confirmed: Aaron Steele."* The door opened and Aaron sighed. He shrugged at me.

"Technology buff," he explained. I nodded. We walked in the foyer of the building and towards the elevator.

"So who is this 'old friend' of yours?" I implored.

"He's someone that I got out of a tight spot a few years ago. I set him up here and I check up on him every once in a while." The elevator stopped on the fourth floor and we stepped outside. Aaron led me to a door and knocked on it. The door opened a crack and I saw a brown eye peer out.

"Okay, it is you," a male voice said in relief. I heard him mess with the chain and then the door opened fully. I saw the person behind the voice and was shocked. It was a boy who was only a few years older than me. He had spiky brown hair and dark brown eyes like my own. He was tall and had ears that stuck out awkwardly. His plaid shirt had a few stains on it and he wore black Chuck Taylors. I still had to smile.

Aaron gently pushed me inside the small apartment. "Jeez Aaron, you could have told me that you were bringing a girl with you!" the boy hissed as he hurried around the room, picking up dirty dishes and pizza boxes and shoving them into the small kitchen.

"Sorry, but I didn't have time. This is August Havens, Jase. She is Conner's daughter."

Jase stopped what he was doing when he heard my father's name. "Why do you have Conner's daughter with you?"

"Wait, you know my dad?" I asked in confusion.

"I know *of* him," Jase replied. "Your dad is a legend. It's an honor to meet you. I'm Jason Beckett, but you can call me Jase." He stuck out his hand for me to shake.

I took it and shook it firmly. "Nice to meet you, Jase. You can call me August."

"August. That's a cool name."

"Thanks," I said while blushing.

"Not to be rude, but why are you here?" he asked gently.

"Um..." I could feel tears growing in the corners of my eyes.

Aaron stepped in for me. He handed me the bag with clothes. "How about you go freshen up? I'll explain the situation to Jase."

I smiled gratefully and went into the other room. I leaned against the door and slid down to the floor. *I will not cry. I will not be afraid.* I put my head in my hands and struggled to keep the tears from flowing down my cheeks. A sob escaped from my lips. I slapped my hand over my mouth and hoped Aaron and Jase hadn't heard me. I pressed my ear against the door to try to hear their conversation.

*"Her parents were just killed last night, Jase. What am I supposed to do about it?"* He sighed. *"I have no idea how to deal with a teenage girl. Conner just dropped a bomb on me."*

*"Aaron, you promised her father that you would look after her. You can't break that promise."*

*"I'm not planning on it. Her face is plastered all over the federal databases. She's a wanted fugitive."*

Not wanting to hear anymore, I turned away and reached into the bag of clothing. I shed my outfit from the previous night and pulled on a pair of jeans and a blue button up shirt. I pulled my long hair up into a high ponytail and wiped away my tears. I was my father's daughter. I would be strong, no matter how scared I was. I held my head up high and walked into the living room. Aaron and Jase looked up when I came in.

"I'm sorry for that little incident," I apologized. "I feel much better now."

"There's no need to apologize," Jase replied. "You have been through a pretty rough night. It's okay to cry."

"I need to keep my emotions in check," I stated. "I can't be reduced to a sobbing mess when we're trying to survive." I was lying through my teeth, but I didn't care.

"So…you have amnesia?" Jase asked. "That's interesting."

"I wouldn't call it that," I argued. "I feel like I'm trapped in my own mind. I can't even remember the most important thing that ever happened to me."

Aaron had been silent during the conversation until now. "August, are you sure you don't remember anything else?"

"Yes," I said in exasperation. "Sometimes I see flashes of the accident, or sounds, but I just can't wrap my mind around what's happening." I rubbed my temples. "I just wish I could remember more."

"You might never recall anything else," Jase put in. "Head injuries are tricky, especially if they're traumatic."

Aaron gave him a look. "Thank you, Jase. I think she's heard enough of your advice."

Jase put his hands up in surrender. "I'm just trying to help."

I ignored them and went to stand by the window. I stared blankly out at the city beyond me. "August, it's not a good idea to stand there," Aaron warned.

"Why?" I asked bitterly. "If a sniper really wanted to kill me, he would have done it by now."

"You don't know that," Aaron countered. "Please, just step back."

In order to alleviate his fears, I obeyed. I took the time to really look at the apartment. It was definitely a bachelor pad. The living room and kitchen were combined and the room was furnished with a brown futon, a soft looking leather recliner, and a blue beanbag chair. A petite entertainment center appeared to be struggling under the weight of the flat screen TV and the extremely unnecessary amount of gaming and sound equipment.

The kitchen was functional. There was a stove, a refrigerator, a microwave, and a tiny sink. I noticed with disgust that the sink was filled with dirty dishes. "Not much of a housekeeper, are you?" I called to Jase.

"No, not really. I'm more of a 'shove it under the bed and hope it disappears' type."

I laughed. "You need a maid."

"If I could afford one, I'd totally get one."

"Why don't you just learn how to clean your own apartment?" I asked with a grin.

"Too lazy," Jase answered.

"That's not an excuse," I replied.

"Well, it's the only one I've got." Jase stood up from the futon. "Why don't you sit down? You've been traveling for hours."

"Fine, I'll stop criticizing your cleaning skills." I sat down on the futon next to Jase. I looked over at Aaron, who was sitting in the recliner. "So what now, Aaron?"

"We have plane tickets for Portugal in the morning. We'll fly there then."

"Portugal? Why Portugal?" I asked in confusion.

"We have to country hop in order to appear less suspicious," Jase explained. "It's a spy trick."

I raised an eyebrow. "Wait, you're coming with us?"

"Of course," Aaron replied. "Jase is under my protection. I can't leave him in the States while we go to Europe. I have to keep an eye on him."

I glanced over at the nerdy boy. I leaned in close to Aaron. "Are you sure about this? Can we trust him?"

"Yes, we can trust him. He's a genius, August. We might need his technological knowhow."

"Okay, I believe you. But if he ends up turning against us, I get to say 'I told you so.'"

"Agreed," Aaron consented. "For now, we need to lay low. We have some long days ahead and we need our rest."

"I can order pizza," Jase suggested. "You guys must be hungry."

"I'm okay with that," I replied. "I'm starving."

"All right, I'll put the order in. Pepperoni okay for everyone?"

"Fine with me," Aaron said. I nodded in agreement. Jase went to call in the order. I walked around the rest of the apartment to entertain myself. Besides the living room and kitchen, the apartment only had a bedroom and a small bathroom.

"Some safe house," I muttered.

"It's not much, but I call it home." I whipped around and saw Jase standing right behind me.

"Gosh, what are you, a ninja?" I gasped. "Don't sneak up on me like that!"

"I only wish I was that cool," he laughed. "Hey, I'm sorry for bringing up your amnesia. I didn't realize it was a sensitive topic."

"It's okay," I replied. "You didn't know. I don't even know how I feel about it half the time. Sometimes it feels as if I've been sucker punched in my stomach and it hurts. But other times it seems like a blessing not to remember probably the most painful moment I've experienced. I'll just need to decide which path to choose: remembering or forgetting."

"Whatever you need August, I can help." He looked at me with his deep brown eyes. "I know you just met me, but we need to depend on each other. You've been through a lot in the past day, but it's going to get a lot worse and you'll need to trust me, all right? I can help you. I've been through a lot of this stuff before."

I didn't really know what to say. I'd never had a guy pour out his heart to me before. "Um, thanks," I said. "I'll keep that in mind." I awkwardly walked away and into the other room.

"Okay. You're welcome," he replied quietly. I glanced behind me and saw him groan and put his head against the wall. I smiled and shook my head.

"I'm not that easy," I whispered. I plopped on the couch. "Anything good on TV?" I asked Aaron, who was vaguely flipping through channels.

"Not much," he answered. "We're not on the news, so that's good. Celia must not want to make a fuss quite yet. She's probably got her men sniffing us out, though."

"Nice to know. So what did Jase do to deserve this tiny box of a safe house?"

Aaron just looked at me blankly. "I can't tell you. It'll have to come from him."

"What are you, the keeper of everyone's secrets?"

"That's right," he replied with a grin.

I laughed. "Well at least you're honest."

"I try my best." Just then, the pizza arrived and Jase went downstairs to pay for it. I made myself busy setting the table and even cleaning some of the dishes in the sink. Then, I found some vegetables in the fridge that weren't totally rotten and used them to make a salad. I placed the salad bowl on the table and grabbed a pitcher of lemonade out of the fridge. Jase walked in right as I put the lemonade down.

"Wow," he said. "That's the best that table has looked since I moved in."

"I couldn't stand to look at it anymore," I joked. "Plus I couldn't let those vegetables go to waste like the rest of them."

"I was planning on cleaning out the fridge," Jase replied weakly.

"Well I did it for you. Besides, it needed it, especially since you're going to be gone for a long time. You aren't going to come back here to a ton of rotten food."

"Thanks." He put the pizza box on the table. "Now let's get started."

Soon we were all diving into the pizza and salad. I hadn't realized how starved I was. The last thing I had eaten was popcorn at the movie the night before. "This is great," I moaned as I swallowed a bite of cheesy goodness.

"Do you want us to leave you two alone?" Aaron laughed.

"No," I managed to say. "I just haven't eaten in forever." I yawned. "Or slept."

"You can have my bedroom," Jase offered. "I can sleep on the floor."

"I don't want to take your bed," I tried to argue.

"No, you need it. It's okay. Go ahead."

"Try to sleep, August," Aaron urged. "You're going to need it." I nodded and walked into the other room. I sat down on the bed and took off my shoes.

*Hopefully I'll be able to sleep.* I lay my head on the pillow. "Please don't haunt my dreams," I whispered. I closed my eyes. Within seconds, I was fast asleep.

~*O*~

I awoke in the passenger seat of a car that was driving at a rapid speed. I looked over at the driver and saw it was my father. "Daddy?" I asked in shock.

"August, stay down!" he ordered. "They're catching up to us. I won't be able to stay ahead of them for long. You have to get out of here."

"No! I'm not leaving you!" I glanced out the window and saw a black SUV chasing our car.

"This seems familiar...but not right," I mused. I turned to my father. "Daddy, why are they chasing us? Why are they after us?"

"You'll find that out eventually. You're smart, August. You're just like your mother. You'll unravel our past someday. But now, you have to go." He unlocked my door.

"No, Daddy! Tell me the truth!" All of a sudden, my door opened and light filled the vehicle.

*"You will find out the truth one day, August Marie."* Just then, I was sucked out of my seat and into the light. I screamed as I was pulled away from my father.

*"No!"* I shrieked. *"Daddy!"*

~*O*~

31

I cried out as I awoke. Gasping for air, I sat there for a moment in an attempt to catch my breath. "Why do you torment me?" I asked breathlessly. "How can I find out the truth?"

The door flew open and Aaron and Jase came running in. "Are you okay?" Aaron asked with his gun drawn. "We heard you screaming."

"I'm fine," I snapped. "I just had a bad dream. Put the gun away. If assassins were coming in after me, they would have had a wakeup call." I pulled a pistol from underneath my pillow. "See?"

"Where did you even get that?" Aaron questioned angrily.

"I found it in your bag," I answered. "I thought I could use it."

"You can't use a gun," he argued. "You're only fifteen."

"My father taught me how to shoot," I explained crossly. "I know how to use one safely."

"That doesn't mean that you can just steal it out of my bag!"

"I have to protect myself somehow!"

"Hey!" Jase yelled. "Both of you, just shut up and stop fighting for one minute!" Aaron and I stopped arguing and looked at him. "Look Aaron, August needs to be able to protect herself. You won't be around all the time to help her. She needs to have some sort of weapon. August, you need to respect Aaron's advice. He's only trying to help you. Like he's told you, he doesn't have to be here. You have to listen to him."

I nodded, though I hated being talked to like I was a child. Aaron leaned against the door. "I agree that she needs a weapon, but it needs to be approved by me. I also have to know that she's able to shoot a gun properly."

I sighed. "I've been shooting since I was thirteen. My dad thought that every woman needed to know how to shoot a gun just in case. I've been going to the shooting range by my house every weekend. I can fire everything from a shotgun to a 9mm pistol. My dad was going to teach me how to shoot his .45 this Saturday." I stammered as I remembered my dad's promise.

Jase's new name was Andrew and I had to pretend that he was my brother. It was a little strange, especially since I had just met him and he seemed interested in me. *That will be awkward if he accidentally says something that implies that he likes me.* Our "father's" name was Cole. To me, this was even stranger. I had just lost my parents and now I had to act like Aaron was my dad.

*"You will never be my father,"* I had told Aaron at the apartment.

*"I'm not asking to be him,"* he had replied. *"I'm just asking you to play along for a few days."* I agreed since I really had no other choice.

I tried not to limp as we made our way to security. Aaron had stopped by a drugstore and bought supplies to bandage my ankle. He had felt it and thought it was a sprain, but couldn't be certain without an X-ray. For now, I had to make do with a brace and some painkillers. We could easily find a swayable doctor in Portugal.

As we stood in line, my palms began to sweat. I had no idea if our plan would work. We might be shut down right here. Aaron and Jase were completely calm as they handed their passports and tickets to the TSA official. He merely glanced at them before giving them back. I gave mine to him and he looked at my photo and back at me. He smiled. "Have a nice flight, Miss Stacey."

"Thank you," I said as I took my passport from him. I followed my companions towards the metal detectors.

"See? It's not that bad," Jase joked.

"I about had a nervous breakdown back there," I retorted.

"It's always hard your first time," he countered. "You get used to it after a while. I can slip on a new identity like a glove."

"That's what I'm afraid of," I whispered.

"Don't get cocky, *Andrew*," Aaron warned. "We're not out of the woods yet. We still have a long way to go."

Jase looked embarrassed and stared at his shoes. I stifled a laugh. I felt bad for him, but he was being a little *too* confident.

We walked through the rest of security with ease and were

soon headed towards our plane. We had booked seats on a private business jet along with some other passengers. Aaron had checked them out and had found nothing out of the ordinary. *Apparently the Stacey family is wealthy,* I thought to myself as we headed towards the tarmac where our plane was waiting.

It was a gorgeous sleek white plane. I gasped as I walked towards it. "It's a Dassault Falcon 900," Aaron explained. "Beautiful, right?"

"Um, yeah," I managed to say. "How many other people are flying this thing with us?"

"Seven, including the pilot and copilot. Don't worry, I know them. They're old friends and are willing to let us tag along. It'll just be some couples and their kids. Don't tell them your real name, though. I don't trust them that much."

I nodded and rolled my suitcase to the staircase into the cabin. A man was instantly there to grab my bag. "Let me, Miss Stacey," he said. I allowed him to carry it into the plane. He repeated the process with Aaron's and Jase's. I climbed to the cabin and was shocked by the luxury of my surroundings. There were plush chairs and couches along the sides of it and soft rich colored carpeting covered the floor.

"Wow," I whispered in wonder. I collapsed onto one of the couches. "So this is how the other half lives."

"Come on Ellie, don't embarrass us," Jase put in. "It's not like you've never been in one of these before. Sam owns a much nicer one."

I took that as a sign that my "family" was wealthy. I sat up straight and smoothed the wrinkles out of my wine red skirt. "Of course. I forgot. Sam's is much better than this."

"Be nice, kids." Aaron put his bag beside a chair. "I don't want to hear you bicker for the next eight hours."

I smiled. "Yes, Dad." It felt so wrong. I bit my lip to keep from crying.

Just then, an older man and a brunette woman came up the stairs into the plane. They were wearing business attire and carrying briefcases. The woman grinned. "You must be Mr.

Stacey," she said as she shook Aaron's hand. "I'm Allison Crosway, and this is my husband David." The man shook Aaron's hand as well.

"Call me Dave," he said robustly. "We're friends with Neil and Elizabeth."

"Yes, of course. They've mentioned you once or twice," Aaron replied politely. "I'm Cole, by the way. These are my children, Andrew and Eleanor. Stand up and be polite."

I gave my hand to Allison. "Please call me Ellie. Eleanor was my grandmother's name."

"It's nice to meet you, Ellie. Help yourselves to any snacks, kids. It's a long flight and it will be a while before lunch."

Jase didn't think twice before diving into a basket of goodies on a table. I decided to wait and sat down at another table. Aaron joined me. "We'll take off once Neil and Elizabeth and their son gets here," he said.

"Cool," I replied. I opened my bag and pulled out a magazine. I flipped through the pages, but couldn't really absorb any information. It was just a gossip rag anyway. It wasn't like there was anything wholesome to learn. "Who are Neil and Elizabeth again?"

"They are old friends of mine. I saved their son from kidnappers ten years ago. Neil's a powerful politician and they took young Matthew for leverage. I rescued him and they promised to fulfill a favor for me whenever I needed to use it, no matter how illegal it was. I'm cashing it in now."

"Good friends," I said in awe. "Do they know who Andrew and I are?" I used Jase's fake name in case Allison and Dave were listening.

"No, not exactly. They think that you and Andrew are brother and sister and that I'm taking you to a safe house in Portugal since the government kidnapped your parents. I can't tell them who you really are in case they're caught and tortured."

"Oh," I answered.

The door opened and another couple stepped inside along

with a young man. They were older, and I noticed the man's eyes were dark and cold. He stared at me before smiling. My stomach churned. *Something's not right.*

I looked at Aaron and noticed that his face was stark white. "What's wrong?" I managed to say around the lump in my throat.

"That's not Neil, Elizabeth, and Matthew," he replied quietly. "They're imposters."

All of a sudden, I heard a thump. Jase had fallen onto the floor unconscious. "Andrew!" I cried as I ran to his side. The door of the plane slammed shut and we began to move. The sudden movement knocked us to the ground. I turned to Aaron. "What is going on?" I asked in terror. He had a blank look on his face and I realized he had no idea.

"Hello, August," the strange man spoke. "It's nice to finally meet you. My name is Agent Thomas. I'm with the FBI. I've been ordered to bring you in."

I felt someone dragging me to my feet. A knife was held to my throat. I flinched at the cold steel against my skin. "I don't know what you're talking about," I said fearfully. "My name is Eleanor Stacey. What did you do to my brother?" I saw my captor was none other than Dave.

"What did you do to the Graysons?" Aaron ordered coldly.

"They're...otherwise detained, Mr. Steele," Agent Thomas replied. "Now unless you want the girl hurt, you'll surrender peacefully."

I felt the knife being pressed against my skin. "I don't think he's joking!" I gasped.

Aaron shook his head. "Celia wants her alive. She'll send you to a bunker in Siberia if you hurt her. Maybe even worse."

"Aaron..." I pleaded as the knife cut slightly into my skin.

"You should have eaten the food," Dave said. "You'd be passed out like Sleeping Beauty over there."

*They drugged Jase,* I realized in horror. *They were going to drug me. They would capture us while we were unconscious and kill Aaron in order to prevent him from going after us.*

"It's okay, August," Aaron put in calmly. He reached into his waistband and pulled out a pistol. He held it up where Thomas could see it.

"Put it on the ground and kick it to me," the agent ordered. His "wife" had a gun pointed at Aaron's chest. Allison had a similar one pointed to his back. Aaron complied and Thomas picked up the gun. He stuck it in his own waistband. "Cuff her," he told Dave. "We can't have them moving around all the way to Europe."

"Europe, huh?" Aaron said. "Not Langley?"

"We can't kill you here, Steele," Thomas explained. "But we can kill you in a car crash in Portugal."

Goosebumps prickled my arms as Dave dragged me to a chair. He cuffed my wrists to the arms of it and I winced when he snapped the restraints a little too tightly. Aaron was restrained across the aisle from me and Jase was placed in a sitting position in another chair and also cuffed.

"You're never going to win," I hissed at the FBI agent. "You're going to lose."

"We'll see about that, Miss Havens. I'm to escort you to our Lisbon base where you are meeting with Director Keene. Mr. Beckett has a plane waiting to take him to his new lab. Mr. Steele, you already have a spot reserved in either a Russian prison or a runaway car. You decide. I'll leave you all to say your goodbyes. We land in eight hours." Thomas walked up to the cockpit.

I looked at Aaron. "What did they do to your friends?"

"Probably killed them," he answered bluntly. "Most likely, he kidnapped them and tortured them until they knew our location. Anyone who can see my file knows that I helped them. So he got to them before I could."

"I'm sorry," I said. "They seemed like nice people."

"Thanks, August. Why don't you get some rest? You won't be able to get much once we land."

"No way. I can't sleep tied up. Besides, I need to keep an eye on Jase." I glanced over at the nerdy boy. "He has a lab?"

"Jase can tell you about it sometime." He leaned over towards me. "Don't lose faith, August. We will get out of here."

"I'm sorry, but I think our luck is about to run out," I answered mournfully.

Aaron smiled. "Oh, ye of little faith." He turned back to his chair. I noticed that Allison and Dave (if those were even their real names) had been put on guard duty. They both had their hands on their guns as if ready for attack. *How did they expect us to do so handcuffed?*

I stared in silence out the window. *How did I get myself into this mess?*

~\*O\*~

A few hours later, we were flying smoothly over the Atlantic. I had resigned myself to my fate. It was no use struggling. In a matter of hours, I would be in Celia Keene's custody and she would do whatever she wanted. Aaron had remained calm this whole time and taken a small nap.

Jase stirred in the seat beside me. He opened his eyes slightly. "August?" he asked hoarsely.

"I'm right here," I replied.

"What happened?" he groaned. "Oh, my head."

"They drugged you," I explained. "The CIA caught up to us."

"Of course they did." He sat up straight. "I escaped them for two years but it seems my luck ran out."

"Two years?" I asked in shock.

"Yeah. I don't want to talk about it."

I turned to Aaron. "Aaron," I said.

"Yeah?"

"You have to tell me who I really am," I pleaded. "Face it, we're not going to make it to Europe. I'm never going to see my father's box. He won't be able to tell me the truth. I'd rather know who I am before I'm forced into service. I can't go in there without knowing my story."

Aaron smiled. "Do you really not have that much faith in me?"

I gave him a strange look. "How do you expect to escape? We're in an airplane surrounded by armed men. They'll kill you if you try anything."

"It's our best shot, August," Jase put in.

"All right, I'll join this suicide mission," I said in exasperation. "I'd rather die than be forced to join the CIA."

"That's the spirit," Aaron replied. "August, are you good with distractions?"

I grinned. "Of course." I turned towards the agents who were guarding us. "Excuse me, but I need to use the restroom. Can I please go?" I requested innocently.

They looked at each other before nodding. "Come with me," Allison said. I glanced at Aaron, who gave me a small nod.

"You can do this," he whispered.

The woman unlocked me from my handcuffs and I quietly stood. We walked towards the back of the plane. "So you want me to become one of you?" I asked. "Lovely."

"It's not that bad, Miss Havens. "It's actually a great opportunity."

*Great opportunity, my rear end.* "Thank you for the reassurance," I replied. I slipped into the bathroom and smiled when I looked at the gun I had taken from her. "All right Aaron, what do you want me to do now?" I mused as I hefted the gun. Then, it hit me. "This is going to suck," I groaned. "Dad, please forgive me for what I'm about to do."

*You want a distraction, Aaron? I'll give you a distraction.* I flushed the toilet and splashed water on my face. "This is it. Be strong." Slipping the gun in my waistband, I walked calmly out of the room. The agent placed a hand on my shoulder.

"It will all be over soon, Miss Havens."

"That's what I'm afraid of," I said softly. I pulled away from her and stuck the gun to my head.

The five agents immediately stopped what they were doing and pointed their guns at me. I took a shuddering breath.

"August..." Aaron warned. "What are you doing?"

"You want me, right?" I asked. "I'm the 'final piece', remember? So you can't shoot me. If you kill me, you'll lose whatever you want from me. But if you don't free my friends right now, I swear I will put a bullet in my brain. You'll lose your final piece, and I'll be able to see my parents again. It's not a horrible decision, really. Besides, you won't have to keep up that flimsy coma story anymore."

"Miss Havens, put down the gun," Agent Thomas ordered. "We don't want to hurt you."

"No!" I yelled. "I am not some soldier that you can order around. I am done with being a piece in your game." With a trembling finger, I flipped off the safety. "I will kill myself. Now release Aaron and Jase!"

"August, no!" Jase cried.

"August, your father would not have wanted this," Aaron put in calmly.

"I don't care. I don't want to live anymore." I put my finger to the trigger. I closed my eyes and breathed in deeply. "Goodbye." I opened one eye a little bit and smiled when I saw Aaron pick his final lock. "Catch!" I yelled as I threw the gun to him. All of the agents, Thomas included, looked at Aaron in shock.

"Well done," Aaron told me.

"Thanks."

"How do you possibly expect to get out of this, Steele? You're surrounded," Thomas said smugly. "There's no way out."

"That's where you're wrong," I said. "Aaron is like Houdini. You can't contain him." With that, I kicked a gun out of Dave's hand. I grabbed it and pointed it at the man I had just incapacitated.

"So we'll have a Mexican standoff until we reach the States? Not a smart idea, Steele."

"Right now, it's the only one I've got."

I was thinking about the odds. Seven people, including the

pilot and copilot, against Aaron, Jase, and me. I could probably get a couple of shots off, but then Aaron and I might be killed or captured. "Aaron, we have to do something."

"I know, just let me think."

"Well, think harder!" I cried. My hand was shaking and it was becoming harder to hold my gun steady.

"It's over, Steele," Thomas ordered. "Hand over the girl and I'll think about not shooting you here."

"Not a chance," I said angrily as I pointed my gun at him. "The only way I'm leaving this plane with you is in a body bag."

"Unfortunately that's not an option, Miss Havens. We have strict orders to bring you back alive."

"That's not going to be possible," Aaron countered. "She is coming with me." He looked straight at me. "August, duck," he whispered.

My eyes grew wide. Quickly, I dove onto the floor. I saw Aaron slam Thomas's head into the overhead compartment and then bullets began to fly. I screamed and covered my head. I heard Jase start yelling. *He's still tied up*, I realized in horror. I lifted my head from the floor and started to crawl towards where Jase was sitting.

"What are you doing?" he said over the sound of gunfire.

"Saving your life," I grunted. I pulled a bobby pin out of my hair and began picking the lock on his handcuffs. "Is Aaron all right?" I said.

"Yeah, he's fine. He just shot someone."

"Good." I kept messing with the lock. "Keep your head down."

"No August, I want to get shot in the face," he replied sarcastically.

"Shut up," I replied. I pulled off the handcuffs. "I'm going to go help Aaron. You stay here, all right?"

"It's too dangerous," he warned. "You could get killed."

"If I die, at least the CIA loses," I said grimly. I cocked my pistol and crawled towards the firefight. I was about halfway in the aisle when someone grabbed me by the hair and dragged me from the row. I shrieked and fought my attacker. My pistol was kicked from my hand and I was hoisted to my feet. I felt the muzzle of a gun in the back of my shoulder.

"The director may want you alive, but she didn't say how alive," Agent Thomas threatened in my ear. I tensed up. Bullets stopped flying and I saw Aaron look up in shock. "Give up, Steele," the man commanded. "Unless you want this girl to have a bullet scarring her pretty face." I stared at Aaron hopelessly. He gave me a small nod.

"Okay," I mouthed. I elbowed my captor in the stomach and hit the deck. I left Aaron to take care of the rest. Not wanting to see another man get killed, I began to crawl towards the front of the plane. Then, I heard my own name. "Why do you want August?" Aaron ordered angrily. "Tell me!"

A bullet flew over my head and into the man's forehead. I screamed and hid in one of the empty aisles. I looked over and saw a dead body beside me. I realized it was Agent Thomas's "wife." I threw a hand over my mouth to prevent from crying out. *Don't freak out. She's dead. She can't hurt you.* I peered out and realized that Aaron was unarmed and the pilot was shooting at him. I saw a gun clutched in the dead woman's hand and grimaced. "Ew, ew, ew," I moaned as I pulled her cold fingers off it. "Aaron, gun!" I cried as I slid it towards him. He caught it at once, leaned out into the aisle, and shot twice in rapid succession. The pilot fell over, dead. I gasped in relief.

"Oh, thank God. I'm still alive." I checked my body for gunshot wounds, but thankfully found none. Aaron had already walked up to the cockpit and was pushing a few buttons. I followed him. "Are you okay?" I implored.

"August, do you know how stupid that was?" Aaron answered coldly.

"What, sliding you a gun?"

"No, almost committing suicide right in front of everyone!"

I recoiled. "You asked for a distraction!" I accused. "I gave you a pretty good distraction!"

"August, you can't keep putting yourself in danger like this.

You could have died and there was nothing I could have done to stop it. Your father and mother meant for you to live. You need to start listening to me."

I glared at him. "I didn't even know you existed until three days ago. You are not my father and you never will be. Please leave me alone."

Aaron straightened. "All right, you can stay in here. I need to talk to Jase anyway. You can make sure the plane stays in the air since you obviously know how to take care of yourself." He left the cockpit and slammed the door behind him. I stood in shock and horror.

"Aaron!" I wailed while trying not to step on the dead pilot.

He opened the door. "Yes, August?"

"I don't know how to fly a plane!" I cried.

He smiled. "You're thirty thousand feet in the air. It's not like you're going to hit anything. Besides, I already put it in autopilot. Just stay here." He left again.

"Don't you dare leave me in here with these dead bodies!" I yelled. "You jerk!" I tried to open the door, but found it locked. "Aaron Steele, let me out!" I sighed and leaned against the wall. All of a sudden, the dead copilot fell out of his seat on top of me. I screamed and pushed him off.

Aaron and Jase walked in right as I was pulling myself out from underneath the copilot. "Having fun?" Jase asked with a raised eyebrow.

"No," I replied in frustration. "I'm stuck in here with two dead bodies!" Aaron offered me a hand and I reluctantly took it.

"You have to trust me to keep you safe, August," he said. "Everything I do, I do to protect you."

"I still don't know you," I answered. "I don't know anything about you."

He sighed. "It's better that way." He adjusted the controls. "Trust me, August."

I walked out of the cockpit and into the main cabin. Jase followed me. "Don't worry, he's always that way. I received the same speech when he saved me."

45

I glanced at the nerdy boy. "Who are you, Jason Beckett? What made you go on the run?"

Jase rubbed the back of his head and looked at the ground. "It's a very long and complicated story, I'm afraid. I don't really want to talk about it." He sat down in one of the empty seats. "Have you remembered anything else?"

"No," I answered. "Please stop asking. I will tell you if I do, I promise." I leaned against a chair across the aisle. "Can you tell me anything about who you are?"

"Let's just say that I used to work for the CIA until I came across something... No matter how important you are to your country, you can always be disposed." He smiled. "What about you, August Havens? Anything interesting about you?"

"I'm afraid not. I'm just a normal teenage girl who was living in Philadelphia until my parents died. Then, I find myself being chased and threatened with guns along with having to trust two strange men who I've never met, but claim to know my father. I guess that's a little interesting, right?" I laughed.

"Yeah, that is," Jase replied. "I'm surprised you've stuck around this long."

"I don't really have any other choice," I said. "It's either being stuck with you two or captured by the CIA." I smiled. "So far this seems like the better option."

Jase laughed. "You are definitely the most interesting girl I've ever met."

"I'm glad you think so," I said with a grin.

"Buckle up!" Aaron yelled from the cockpit. "We're going to land soon, and it's not going to be pretty!"

I instantly sat down and buckled my seatbelt. Jase did the same. I clutched onto my seat rests in fear. I felt a hand on mine. I looked over and saw Jase holding my hand. "It's going to be all right," he said reassuringly over the roar of the engine.

"I hope you're right!" I replied. We felt the plane falling forward into a steep incline. I squeezed my eyes shut and hoped for the best. *Mom, Dad, at least I'll see you soon.*

Just then, the plane leveled out. From the window I could

see we were flying over grassy meadows and a few farms. "We're landing here?" I asked. "Why not at an airport?"

"There would be agents waiting for us there," Jase explained. "If we land here, it will give us some time to get away."

"Oh." The plane shook manically. "We're going to crash, aren't we?"

"I would call it more of an unplanned landing...but yeah it's technically a crash."

"Great," I groaned. I grabbed his hand and bit my lip.

"August, if we die, I want you to know something."

"No, you are not going to talk like that!" I ordered. I gasped as my ears popped from the pressure changes. "We are not going to die! There's still a way out of this."

The plane slowed in its descent and I breathed a sigh of relief. "August..." Jase said.

"Can I have my hand back, please?" I asked. He reluctantly let go of my hand and I placed it back in my lap. We felt the wheels touch the ground and then we were thrown forward without dignity. "Ouch," I moaned as I rubbed where my head had smacked the seat in front of me.

"Are you okay?" Jase put in with concern.

"Yeah, I'm fine. It just stings a little."

"August, you're bleeding."

"It's fine." I waved him away. "Aaron?" I called.

"Is everyone alive back there?" he yelled back.

"Barely!" Jase shouted. "That was a bit of a close call!"

Aaron leaned out of the cockpit with a big grin on his face. "That's what makes it fun," he replied. "Now let's go. The authorities will be on us in no time. Once Thomas doesn't check in, they'll assume we escaped."

I stood up and grabbed my bag. "Well, let's not just stand here. Let's go!"

After grabbing our bags from the baggage compartment, Jase, Aaron, and I climbed out of the wreckage and into a peaceful meadow. I gasped as I landed into the tall grass that tickled my legs. "Where are we?" I said in awe.

"Portugal. About a few hours away from Lisbon. I have a contact there that will help us get to Switzerland."

"Can we trust them?" I asked.

"She's the best in her field. If she can't help us, no one can."

"'She,' huh?" Jase put in. "Is this one of your conquests, Aaron?"

"No," Aaron said bluntly. "I helped her out of a tough spot like I did with you. She owes me a favor."

"Hopefully she's true to her word," I replied while adjusting my bag on my shoulder.

"She will be," Aaron agreed. "I'm the reason she's alive."

I raised an eyebrow, but said nothing. *He has a history with this woman, whoever she may be.* Aaron began walking towards a small highway, so Jase and I followed.

"August, can we talk about what happened on the plane?" Jase asked cautiously.

"What is there to talk about? It was a tense moment where we thought we were about to die. You said the first thing that popped into your head. I stopped you. Nothing happened, Jase. Even if anything did, I'm nowhere near ready to have a relationship. I just lost my parents and I'm trying to stay one step ahead of our enemies." I began to walk faster to catch up to Aaron.

"Okay," I heard him say faintly. "If that's how you feel."

I looked down at the ground. *I don't mean to break your heart. I just can't deal with this right now.*

"Come on, you two." Aaron's voice broke my thoughts. "We have to get to the city before the authorities show up."

I quickened my pace. Aaron was right. We had to be fast. As we walked, I heard a car coming behind us. I got into the ditch to avoid being hit. The vehicle came screeching to a halt beside us. "Run!" Aaron yelled. I pushed Jase forward and took off.

"Go!" I screamed. I ran as fast as my legs would allow. There was a sharp pain in my ankle and I stumbled and fell into the grass. Someone grabbed my waist and hefted me to my feet. "Aaron!" I cried.

*"August!"* he called as he ran towards me. "No!"

I was thrown inside the car's backseat. "Let go of me!" I shrieked. "Aaron!" The door was slammed shut.

*"¡Vá!"* my captor ordered. The car sped away. I started kicking and fighting the man holding me. Then I felt a needle sting my arm and everything faded to black.

# 5

*Unknown Location*

I opened my eyes and saw nothing but darkness. *What the...*
The last thing I remembered was being forced into a car by a
strange man. *There's another memory lost.* "Hello?" I called
hoarsely.

"Hello, August." Something was whipped off my head and
bright light shone into my eyes. I focused and saw it was
someone shining a flashlight in my eyes.

"Who are you?" I ordered. "Where am I? I'm getting sick
and tired of being knocked unconscious and waking up in
strange places." I saw the figure of a man with hands clasped in
front of him sitting across a table from me. I tried to move my
arm to get my hair out of my face, but it was tied to the arm of
the chair I was sitting in. *Wait, what?* My eyes snapped into
focus. A man in his early thirties looked back at me. He was
Hispanic, with dark brown eyes and a goatee.

"I see the drugs are wearing off," he said. "Good to know."

"Who are you?" I snarled.

"I am *Santiago Mario Montoya Vicario,*" he told me with a

flourish. "But pretty ladies call me Santiago."

I glared at him. "Do some call you 'dirtbag'? Why did you take me in the first place?"

He laughed. "Don't test me, August. As of now, I hold your life in my hands."

I continued to glare. "Where are Aaron and Jase?"

"You have spirit. I like that in a woman."

"I'm fifteen, you creep. So keep your charms to yourself. Now where are Aaron and Jase? Did you take them when you took me?"

"So you don't know that Aaron Steele and Jason Beckett escaped?"

"They escaped?" Relief flooded me. *They got away.*

Santiago pushed a photo across the table to me. "A security photo taken today at the Lisbon train station. As you can see, your companions are very much alive."

I stared at the photo. It was of Aaron and Jase getting on a train. Aaron was glancing behind him as if searching for any tails. Jase was keeping his face forward, but I noticed that he looked worried. *He's probably thinking about me,* I thought. "What do you want with me?" I asked coldly.

"You are a very important girl, Miss Havens. Your government is paying a great deal of money for you. But my government is searching for Aaron Steele. I work for the *Sistema de Informacoes da Republica Portuguesa,* or the Intelligence System of the Portuguese Republic. It's basically Portugal's version of the CIA. Your Mr. Steele stole some very important information from us a few years ago. We want him back. You're the only person who knows where he's going. So August, tell me…where are your companions heading? If you comply it will make things a lot easier."

I gave a sweet smile. "If I tell you, I'll have to kill you."

"You're testing my patience, Miss Havens. That's a bad place to be."

"Well I'm not telling you, dirtbag. I know you won't kill me since I'm the piece to your puzzle. So my lips are sealed."

Santiago seemed as if he was trying to keep from strangling me. "Then I guess we're going to have to do this the hard way." He leaned out the door and made a hand motion. A man in a black suit wheeling a medical tray came in the room. "Do it," he said. "She's being difficult."

I had a bad feeling about this man and began struggling in my seat. "What is that?" I asked, trying to keep the fear out of my voice.

"It's a new potent truth serum my government has developed," Santiago answered. "It hasn't been tested yet. You're the lucky first."

The doctor held up a syringe from the tray. I began to squirm. I hated needles. For years I'd had to get my arm numbed before I got a shot. "I won't tell you anything," I said boldly.

"It seems that you will be the perfect test subject. So, August..." Santiago held the syringe in front of my face. "Will you give me an answer?"

I swallowed hard before glaring at him. "I'd rather die," I said icily.

"I sincerely hope not. But since this drug hasn't been tested before, you might!" I gasped as the doctor grabbed my arm. I felt the sharp sting of the needle entering the crook of my elbow and the burning of the clear liquid inside.

"You jerk!" I cried. My vision began to blur again as the drug took hold. *Come on, stay focused. Don't tell him anything.*

"Now, August...where are your companions heading? I know a smart girl like you would have been told the plan."

Everything within me screamed, *Don't, August! Don't!* Unfortunately, my tongue didn't cooperate.

"Why, Zurich, of course!" I giggled.

Santiago smirked at me evilly. "Thank you very much, August." He turned to the doctor. "Let her sleep it off. I want to know the side effects. After that, kill her. I have no use of her anymore, even if her government wants her so desperately."

"Of course, sir."

Ice water seemed to run through my veins at his words, and I awoke from my trance for a moment. *He's going to kill me,* I thought. *I have to escape or die.* Then I felt as if I was falling and everything blackened.

~\*O\*~

*Langley, Virginia*

Jules fidgeted in her folding chair. She had been alone for what felt like hours. Ever since she had blatantly refused to tell August's location, he had left her by herself in the cold dark room. She was still handcuffed, starving, and really needed to use the bathroom. *I'm not resorting to wetting myself,* she thought.

She wondered about August. She could only hope that she was safe with Aaron and on her way to Europe. *Find your dad's box, cuz. Then get somewhere where these idiots can't find you.*

The door opened and Agent Regan came inside. "Hello, Juliet." He was carrying her purse. He set it down on the table in front of her. "Your sister has been calling you. I think she's worried." He pulled her cellphone out of the bag and put it on the table.

"Let me talk to her," Jules said. "I have to let her know that I'm all right."

"I'm afraid that isn't an option. I can't risk you slipping information to her. But I will drag her in for questioning if you don't start cooperating with us."

"Why would you drag Nat into all of this?" Jules cried. "She knows nothing! August knows nothing! She's just an innocent girl who just lost her parents in a tragic *accident!*"

"That's where you're wrong, Miss Havens. Your cousin isn't as innocent as she seems. She is very special and we need her skills."

Jules' eyes narrowed. "I will never tell you where she is."

Regan smirked. He pulled out a phone from his pocket. "Your cousin is associated with a suspected terrorist. You are now also his accomplice, which is why you're being charged with treason. My words will have your sister arrested for the same charges. Except with her I won't be so nice. She'll be lucky to make it past her first night in jail. Now…" He began to dial a number. "…will you give me an answer?"

Jules was torn. *I can't let Natalie get hurt. I'm all she has in this world.*

"If it helps your decision, I'll also have that fiancé of hers brought in. This is your last chance."

She glared at the federal agent. "You're asking me to decide which one of my family members I want you to kill."

"We won't kill August. She is an important asset."

"You'll kill her soul," Jules replied coldly.

"If you want to think of it that way, go ahead. Just give me a name, Juliet."

She swallowed hard and chose her words carefully. "Vienna," she finally said. "They're going to Vienna. I don't know where. I just know that they're going there."

"Thank you. That wasn't so hard, was it?"

"Let me talk to my sister," Jules ordered.

"I don't think so. I'll be back soon. I have to talk to my superiors." Regan left the room and Jules let out a deep breath. She had managed to fool them, at least for now. Maybe they'd believe her and give August a few more days of freedom.

She thought of Natalie. Her sister was her last surviving family member beside August. Their mother had died giving birth to Nat, and then their father had passed away from leukemia when Jules was nineteen. She gave up any hope of finishing college and devoted her life to Nat through junior high and high school. It was a rough five years, but they managed to survive. They even got scholarships to help Nat go to college. Uncle Conner was around some and he helped them out when he could. When he and his wife Lily gave birth to August, it seemed like their lives were finally turning around. Then the Greek tragedy that was the Havens family reared its ugly head again and destroyed Conner's side. Now their only daughter was a fugitive, Jules was in jail, and Natalie had somehow managed to avoid the carnage. *Let's keep it that way.*

The door opened again and Regan appeared. "You're coming with us. August won't be able to resist coming after you." He pulled her up from her chair and yanked her out of the room.

*Maybe I'll be able to get my hands on a phone,* Jules thought hopefully. *I can call Nat and tell her to get out of town.* She was led down a stark white corridor past tons of people who looked at her with contempt. *They think I'm a traitor.*

Regan opened a door to another room. "Wait here for now. Once transport arrives, I'll take you there." He left her alone. Jules surveyed her new surroundings. The room was nicer. There was a small cot along one wall with a thin blanket, a table and chair sat in the middle of the room. It was still painted in a dreary gray, but at least it felt a little more welcoming. There was even a bathroom connected to the main area, which Jules took advantage of.

She came out after doing her business and sat down on the cot. She had no idea what time it was or even if it was light outside. *I really don't care. I'm just exhausted.* She lay down on the cot and closed her eyes. Maybe when she woke up her situation would turn out to be only a dream.

*Lisbon, Portugal*

I slowly opened my eyes and winced as a massive headache overtook me. "What happened?" I murmured. Then I remembered my interrogation and Santiago's order. *They're going to kill me,* I thought in horror. I tried to sit up, but nausea swept through me. I dry heaved. I hadn't eaten in so long that my stomach was empty.

Fighting through my sickness, my eyes adjusted to the dim light. I was lying on my side on a cold concrete floor. The room was empty and light was coming from a small window high on the wall. I shivered and managed to sit up. I drew my knees to my chin. "How am I supposed to get out of here?" I whispered.

There was no way Aaron would be coming for me. He was on a train with Jase. He had to keep Jase safe, not just me. *I can't believe he would abandon me. He made a promise to my father.* I knew Aaron wouldn't break his promise to my dad that easily. He wouldn't dare leave me behind without a plan of some kind. *It looks like I'll have to come up with a plan of my own.*

I stood and went to the door of my cell. It was locked. I walked across the room to the window. I sighed when I saw that it was made of security glass. Plus, it looked out to an empty alley with no one to see my plight. "Great," I groaned. I leaned against the wall. "If you are going to kill me, just get it over with," I said aloud.

All of a sudden, the door swung open and a slim figure dressed in all black came inside. I couldn't even see the person's face since it was covered with a hood. I almost broke down in tears. "Please, no," I begged. "I'm only fifteen. I can't die now."

My executioner didn't seem to care. They simply strapped handcuffs around my wrists and led me from the room. I swallowed hard as we went down gloomy hallways filled with identical rooms. I could hear screams coming from some of them. "I'm friends with Aaron Steele," I said shakily. "He'll be coming for me. I don't think he'll be happy if I'm dead when he gets here." I tried to sound confident.

The person leading me remained silent. We reached a door which pushed open. There was a black SUV waiting in the alley. I looked back at the figure. They nodded for me to get in. I awkwardly pulled open the door to the backseat and got inside. Just then, I heard voices yelling in a foreign language. Two men came running outside with guns pointed at us. My "captor" swore and jumped into the driver's seat.

"Stay down!" she screamed. I caught a noticeable British accent. She threw the car in reverse and sped out of the alley. I dove onto the floor as the men began shooting at us.

"Who are you?" I cried as the woman turned onto a busy

street.

"A friend," she replied. "That's all you need to know."

"This is Aaron's doing?" I asked.

"Yes." She pulled off her hood, revealing long black hair. "He contacted me right before he left town. I managed to get him identification before coming to rescue you. Sorry for giving you a fright, but I needed to seem legitimate. Apparently I wasn't good enough. I was never great at the whole field agent thing. Give me a laptop and an office any day."

"You're Aaron's contact!" I said in shock. "The woman he saved!"

She looked back at me. "He told you about Barcelona?"

"No," I answered. "Only that he helped you out of a tight spot and you owed him a favor."

She laughed. "He owes me. I've helped him out of many a tight spot as well. I'm Kara Jacobs, by the way. Sorry for not introducing myself properly before, but I was trying to avoid getting shot. I would shake your hand, but I'm driving."

"I'm…"

"August Havens. Daughter of the recently deceased Conner and Lily Havens, cousin of Juliet and Natalie Spencer, and companion of Aaron Steele and Jason Beckett. You're fifteen years old, born in Philadelphia, Pennsylvania, and the youngest person I know to have a five million dollar bounty on her head."

"Five million…wait, how did you know all of that?"

"Aaron told me. He couldn't save you, so he sent me." She brushed her hair behind her ear. "I'm supposed to help you get out of the country and to Germany. You'll board a train and meet up with Aaron and Jase from there. They'll have a bit of a head start, but you should be able to catch them in the Alps."

I nodded. "So who is that Santiago guy? He said he was with the government."

Kara scoffed. "He's not. Santiago Vicario is one of Europe's most wanted. He's an arms dealer. The problem is, he's super rich and has managed to pay off most of the authorities; even made a deal with the CIA to overlook some charges in exchange for you. Unfortunately for them, he wasn't going to keep his end of the bargain. Luckily I got there in time."

"Thank God you did." I was starting to realize how much danger I was in. "Why did he want me dead anyway?"

"Trying to get to Aaron, I think. Giving him a warning."

"What is his problem with Aaron?"

"Aaron was undercover in his operation with the CIA for two years. He double-crossed Santiago and now he wants him dead. He'll stop at nothing until Aaron's head is on a silver platter. Killing you would have shown Aaron he meant business."

"So someone else threatens my life. Great." I pulled myself off the floor and onto the seat.

"You're pretty popular, August. I saw the wanted poster on the federal database. You're on everyone's radar."

"Yay. That's just what I need." I looked out the window at the city. "So how do you tie into all of this?"

"I was involved with Santiago's business for a while for my agency. When Aaron left, I was caught in the crossfire. He came back and managed to rescue me." She smiled. "We've been connected ever since."

I raised an eyebrow. "Really?"

"No, not in that way!" she cried. "He's way too old for me. We're just friends. I help him out and he helps me when he can. He's the reason I'm an agent. But that's another story." She reached into a bag and pulled out a black hood. "Put this on," she ordered. "I can't have you knowing where my base is."

I reluctantly took the hood from her and placed it on my head. "Joy," I muttered.

"Don't worry, I do this to everyone. Even Aaron doesn't know. I usually kidnap him at a random location in Lisbon." I laughed at the thought of Aaron being "kidnapped" by Kara. "See? It's not that bad," she said.

I felt the car begin to slow down. Soon, it stopped and I heard Kara's door open. She pulled open my door and helped me climb out. "We're going up some stairs," she explained. I stumbled a little as I awkwardly found the stairs. She caught my arm and led me up the staircase. "I warned you," she laughed.

"You try walking around with a bag on your head," I retorted.

I heard Kara mess with some keys and then a door opened. She gently pushed me inside and shut it. "You can take the bag off now," she said. I did at once and gulped in fresh air.

"Much better," I breathed. My eyes adjusted to the bright light of the room and I realized that I was in a small apartment. I was standing inside a homey looking living room with modern furniture. I sat on a black and white sofa and looked at my new ally. "Well…now what?" I asked.

"Now I make you look pretty," she answered. "Not that you aren't pretty. In fact, you're quite beautiful. I just need to make you look different enough so Santiago and the government don't recognize you." She walked into an adjoining room. "Do you want to be a brunette or a redhead?" she wondered.

I thought about it for a moment. "Brunette," I replied.

"All right, come in here so I can get to work." I followed her voice and found myself in a small hair salon. My eyes must have been wide because she laughed again. "Being a secret agent has its perks," she explained. I sat down in a salon chair and Kara began to wash my hair. Thirty minutes later, she had trimmed my split ends, applied chestnut brown dye, and gave me blue contact lenses to wear. I gasped when I looked at myself in the mirror. "Pretty sweet, huh?" she asked. "It's amazing what a pair of contact lenses and some hair dye can do."

"I can't believe it," I whispered as I felt my new brown tresses.

"It's a special dye. It won't come out until you use this shampoo." She held up a bottle. "Here's your new identification." She gave me a shiny new U.S. passport and tickets. "Your name is now Lindsey Katherine Fenwick. Your parents died when you were a small child and you were sent to Portugal to live with your uncle. However, he had no idea what to do with a teenager so he is sending you to a boarding school in Switzerland. That should be able to help you get through customs. You're going to board a flight to Paris with a layover in Madrid. Then you will get on a train that takes you to Berlin and then another train to Zurich. Aaron and Jase will find you from there."

I was given clothes to appear inconspicuous. It was simple and consisted of blue jeans, a plain white long sleeved shirt, and a pale blue short sleeved shirt over top of the first. I put on black Chuck Taylors and a pair of black framed glasses. Kara pulled my hair into a messy bun and stuck two silver chopsticks into the bun. "If you take off the tips and stab someone with them, the drug inside will knock them out in minutes," she explained.

I involuntarily shuddered. "That seems dangerous."

"It won't kill them or anything," she countered. "They'll just have a long nap."

I nodded and fingered one of the weapons. "What else do you have?" I asked with a grin.

Kara went over to a closet and threw it open. I gasped when I saw what was inside. "Whatever you need," she replied.

I walked to the closet and fingered the various weapons on the shelves. "Where do we start?" I smirked.

# 6

*En route to Lisbon Portela Airport*

I stared down at my newly painted nails. I hardly ever wore nail polish, but Kara had insisted. I traced the small blue and white vertical stripes in the design to try to ease my nerves. In a matter of minutes, I would be at the airport, then security. How in the world could I explain why I had poison chopsticks, two knives, and a gun hidden on my person plus one suitcase?

Swallowing hard, I turned to Kara. She was focused on making sure no one was following us to the airport. "Are you sure that everything is hidden?" I asked.

"Trust me August, everything is going to be fine. The airport security is stupider than they look. As long as you appear calm, they aren't going to suspect anything. If you start panicking, they will search you."

I nodded. "What do I do if I get caught?"

She sighed. "August, once you get out of this car, you're on your own. I can't help you anymore. You will have to use that brain of yours to figure it out. If you can get to that plane, you'll be home free. If you do get in trouble, I left money in your bag to bribe if necessary. Portuguese customs are harder to bribe, but with the right amount they might let you through. It all depends on the official."

By then, we had driven up to the airport's drop off. Kara put the car in park and my heart began to pound. "Thank you...for everything," I said. "Hopefully I will see you again someday."

"If I did my job right, you shouldn't," she answered. "Best wishes. Good luck, August."

I smiled. "You too, Kara." I got out of the car and grabbed my suitcase from the back seat. I adjusted my shoulder bag and held my head high. It was time for me to escape.

~*O*~

As I walked towards security, I tried to breathing normally. My palms were sweating like they were the time before. *Just breathe, August. If you look calm, they are not going to question you.* I had already checked my suitcase containing a gun and two knives and so far my name hadn't been called. I took that as a good sign.

I put my carryon bag on the conveyor belt and smiled at the security officer standing by the metal detector. I took off my belt and shoes and placed them in a bin. Luckily the chopsticks were ceramic and could stay in my hair. I calmly walked through the metal detector. I quietly put on my things and got my bag before strolling through the main terminal. "I made it," I breathed in relief.

My flight wasn't scheduled to leave for another thirty minutes, which meant that I had half an hour to twiddle my thumbs and hope that my new alias hadn't been discovered by Santiago and his men or the CIA. I bought a cup of coffee and sat in my boarding area. I had a book in my bag, but I wasn't in the mood or right frame of mind to read anything. I kept an eye on the clock. *Come on, move faster,* I pleaded.

Finally, I decided to close my eyes and focus on the accident again. *Was my dream part of it?* Some lines seemed familiar, but I didn't think that my father had been chased by anyone. Jules said a drunk driver had crashed into our car. *But is that the whole truth?*

"What if it was just an accident?" I whispered. "What if I am going crazy?" The only problem was that I knew I wasn't crazy. The CIA was interested in me for some twisted reason. Aaron knew what that reason was, but wasn't telling me. Jase knew of my father. Celia *knew* my father. *How could they possibly know my father? He was just a business lawyer. He took a ton of business trips until I was thirteen. Then the economy went sour and he lost his job. There was nothing special about my family.*

*"Flight 1201 to Madrid is now boarding,"* a voice announced over the intercom. The message was repeated in a few other languages. I grabbed my things and got in line.

*If they're going to catch you, they would have done it by now. They wouldn't have messed around for half an hour waiting to capture you. Just get on the plane and get out of here.* I handed my boarding pass to the flight attendant. She scanned it before letting me on the plane.

"Have a good trip, *Señorita* Fenwick," she said warmly.

I smiled and walked up the tunnel towards the plane. *I've made it this far. If I'm caught now, they'll have to bring me out in a body bag.* After I entered the plane, I found my seat and sat down. I could feel the stress leaving my body. I sighed with pleasure and closed my eyes. *I can take a nice nap. I haven't slept in so long. Maybe I won't have any bad dreams either-*

"Hi! I'm your seat mate!"

My eyes snapped open at the sound of the strange voice. I turned and saw a girl around my age. She had red hair and gray eyes and was dressed in a pink blouse and khaki pants. I noticed with dread that she appeared to be very perky. *Oh joy.*

"I'm Lindsey," I said with a weak smile as I took the stranger's offered hand.

"I'm Kayla," she replied. "It's so nice to meet you!"

*Why did I have to be stuck next to one of these people?* I groaned internally. "Nice to meet you too."

"This is going to be such a great trip," she gushed. "I'm so glad to sit next to someone my age. On my last flight from

Charleston, I was next to a cranky old man and he was *so* mean. He didn't want to hear any of my stories! He was so boring. I think he was on a business trip."

"Um, that's nice," I answered. *I thought Blaire talked too much. Apparently I didn't realize how lucky I was.*

"Enough about me...where are you from?"

"I'm from America," I explained. "But I've lived here in Lisbon for the past nine years with my uncle. He doesn't know what to do with me anymore so he's sending me to boarding school in Switzerland."

"How *awful!*" Kayla cried. "He's just sending you away, without a reason?"

"He says he doesn't know how to handle a teenage girl," I replied. I hoped that would shut her up.

"What about your parents? Where are they?"

I sighed. I really didn't want to mention my parents. "They're dead," I stated bluntly. I didn't mean to be so coarse, but I couldn't say anything more without breaking down in tears.

"Oh." She put her hands over her mouth. "I'm so sorry. I didn't mean to pry."

"It's okay." I was biting my lip to keep from crying. *Just drop it,* I begged.

"Um...to which school are you going?" she asked.

"The Institute Montana in Zugerburg," I answered honestly. *Technically, it's not a lie. I am going to Zurich, which is nearby.*

"That's so crazy!" Kayla exclaimed. "I'm going there too!"

"Oh yay," I said with mock enthusiasm. *It's just my luck that I'm stuck next to a girl going to the actual school!*

"I've never been away from home before, and I was so scared about making new friends. But here you are on the same flight as me! It must be a sign or something!"

"I guess," I replied.

Just then, the flight attendants began their spiel about how to escape the plane in case of fire or a crash. They said it in other languages as well. I was happy that it made Kayla was quiet for five minutes and I could remember what Kara had said about the school.

Far too soon, the attendants finished and the pilot came on the intercom. "Hello, everyone. This is your captain speaking. We have a gorgeous day of flying ahead of us. We should be arriving in Madrid by 1:45, which will be plenty of time to make your connecting flights. I hope you have a wonderful flight." He repeated his message a few times in other languages before signing off the intercom and taxing the plane.

"It always makes me nervous to fly," Kayla said. "I never know if we might crash."

"Uh huh." I was more nervous that federal agents might come rushing out of the airport ordering the pilot to stop so they could arrest me. For me, crashing would be the more merciful option. *Don't think like that. You have to get to Zurich and find Dad's box. It's your only chance to find out what happened.*

The plane began to ascend with no signs of armed men chasing. *I'm free. I just have to get to that train.* I had tickets for the train to Berlin at 8:05 that night, which meant I had a two hour wait until my next trip. *Hopefully I can stay out of sight until then.*

We were soon up in the sky high above Lisbon. I had to smile. I had made it out of Portugal. Now I had to get to Paris.

~*O*~

We had been flying towards Madrid for a while when Kayla began her massive amount of questions again. "Do you play any sports?" she asked.

"I run track," I stated.

"Really? That's so cool. I play softball. I love it." She leaned back in her seat. "Wouldn't it be awesome if we were roommates?"

*No! It would not be awesome! If I was your roommate, I would probably either jump out the window or use my chopsticks on you! Wait a minute...that gives me an idea.* I pulled out a crossword book and a pen out of my bag. I opened the book and looked over the clues. "What's another word for 'ask'? It's seven letters." I handed it to her. She thought it over for a second. While she was concentrating on the page, I leaned over and aimed my pen at her coffee cup. A clear, tasteless sedative squirted cleanly into the cup. I scooted back as she looked up.

"Well that's an easy one. It's 'implore.'" I took the book from her and took a drink of my Coke. She followed by taking a big sip of her coffee.

"Thank you," I said. I smiled as Kayla slumped over in her seat. "Thank you for finally shutting up." I adjusted her to a sitting position. The drug would wear off by the time we reached Madrid. The pen wasn't meant to last long. If I wanted to really knock out someone, I would have to use my chopsticks for longer effects. I only hoped that Kayla wouldn't be following me on the train to Berlin. If she was, I didn't know what I would do.

I turned to face the window. The clouds were beneath the plane's wing and looked just like cotton candy swirls. I wanted to reach outside and grab one in my hand to see how it felt. I smiled at the childish wish. *I'm not that innocent girl anymore. All of my innocence vanished along with my memories.*

I tried to focus on the accident. I could vaguely remember glass breaking and my mother screaming. I shivered at the animalistic cry she made. *She was killed almost instantly. I know she didn't say anything to me. My father however...he wasn't so lucky. He lived long enough to warn me of what was to come. What he said, I'm not sure. All I know is he was trying to save me even though he was close to death.* I closed my eyes at the painful memories. I couldn't do this. It still hurt too much to think about my parents' final moments. Plus my head hurt whenever I tried to remember that night. Right now it felt as if a jackhammer was being driven into my skull. I rubbed my temples and sighed.

*They've probably been buried by now. I wasn't even at their funeral. Some daughter I am. I wonder if they got to say goodbye to each other. It would be horrible if they died without saying that they loved one another.* I noticed Kayla's cellphone sitting on her tray table. *She wouldn't mind if I borrowed it, right? It's not like she would miss it.*

66

I picked up the phone and smirked when I saw she had paid to use the plane's WiFi. *Such a waste of money, but at least I can take advantage of it!* I pulled up Google and typed in "Conner and Lily Havens." Sure enough, their obituaries and an article about their funeral popped up on the screen. I clicked on the funeral article first.

*Philadelphia, Pennsylvania*
*June 22, 2013*

*The remains of Conner Robert Havens, 39, and his wife, Lily Maria Havens, 35, were laid to rest today. Two days ago, the couple was killed in a car accident by a drunk driver who ran a red light. They died while en route to the hospital. The lone survivor of the crash was their fifteen year old daughter August, who is still in a coma at this time. Prayer vigils are being held for the young orphan by her classmates and family.*

*Her cousin Natalie Spencer released a statement stating that August had been moved to a special rehabilitation facility for coma patients. August's guardian Juliet Spencer has accompanied her to the facility. The staff refuses to comment or allow visitors. Blaire Pruitt, a friend of August, said that she hopes her friend wakes up soon. "I want her to know that I'm here for her. The doctors said that she doesn't remember the accident or that her parents are dead. Her memory might be even worse when she wakes up. Auggie, I'm willing to help you remember. Wake up soon so we can talk again. I miss you."*

*It is unknown how long August Havens is expected to be in a coma or even if she will wake up at all. Her doctors have said that the girl is not out of the woods. We send our thoughts and prayers out to this beautiful young girl.*

Tears were sliding down my face. I couldn't believe what Blaire had said about me or the paper. *I'm alive!* I wanted to scream. *I'm not in a coma!* I sucked in a breath in an attempt to calm myself down. *Freaking out will not help you right now. You have to remain calm. Do not draw attention to yourself.* I felt my heart rate begin to slow down and my breathing became even. I touched my parents' obituary.

*Conner Robert and Lily Maria Havens*
*1974-2013, 1978-2013*

*Conner and Lily Havens joined the angels in heaven at 9:00 pm on June 20, 2013 after passing away in a tragic accident. The couple had been married for seventeen years. They met while working together on a project for an insurance company in April of 1994. Conner was a lawyer for the company, Lily was a technician. They were married January 8, 1995. Two years later, they gave birth to their only child, August Marie Havens. They moved to Philadelphia to be with family in June of 1999.*

*They were very devoted parents and spent most of their free time with their daughter. Conner played golf on the weekends and Lily chose to be a stay at home mom, which took up most of her time. Conner had a law degree from Harvard while Lily had a degree in computer science from Boston University.*

*Survivors include their daughter August Havens and their nieces Juliet and Natalie Spencer. They were preceded in death by their parents and Conner's brother and sister in law Matthew and Shannon Spencer. They will be greatly missed.*

I turned off the phone and put it back on the tray table. "Why were they taken from me?" I whispered. "I didn't do anything wrong."

~*O*~

*Madrid Barajas International Airport*

I was in a daze as I climbed off the plane. I couldn't focus on anything. *Why did you read about them?* I scolded myself. *You knew it would mess with your head.*

*I had to know,* I replied angrily. *Great, now I'm arguing with myself.* I sighed and went to find a place to sit. I had a few hours until my flight to Paris. Luckily I had managed to avoid Kayla and blend into the crowd. I bought a cup of coffee and sat down at a table to think. As I sipped the bitter drink, I could feel my head begin to clear.

*If only Aaron and Jase were here.* Aaron would probably be sitting and thinking about what our next move would be. Jase would be teasing me and catching glimpses of me when he thought I wasn't looking. *Why was I so harsh with him? It was only a little crush.*

I couldn't help but think of Jules. She was probably dead by now. I knew Aaron said they would keep her alive in hopes that I would go after her, but that was days ago. My cousin was probably in a shallow grave by now. A single tear ran down my cheek. *Don't think about her. If you're going to freak out, don't think about her.* I shook my head to clear it of memories of Jules.

I pulled out a burner phone that Kara had given me. It was only supposed to be used in an emergency since after you used it, you threw it away. I knew what I was about to do was stupid, but I did it anyway. I dialed Aaron's number. I put it to my ear and waited. *Please be all right,* I thought.

*"This is Aaron Steele."*

"Aaron!" I cried a little too loudly. I clapped a hand over my mouth and hoped no one had heard me.

*"I'm sorry, but I have discarded this phone. If you think I'm dumb enough to keep my same number more than two days, then you're dumber than I thought. If you're August, I'm sorry, kid. I couldn't keep this number open very long. We're safe, if that's what you're wondering. Keep moving."* A chipper "beep" came on over the phone.

*Maybe he can still receive messages.* "Aaron? Aaron, it's me, August. I'm alive. I'm…I'm safe. I got away. Your contact helped me get out of the country. I'm coming for you, you hear me? I'm not going to let you and Jase have all the fun. You wait for me, understand? I'm not going anywhere." I hung up then in case anyone was tracing the call. I quietly took my napkin and wiped my fingerprints from the phone. Then I tossed it in the nearest trash can. "Try finding me now," I whispered.

~*O*~

Aaron Steele had to grin as he heard August's message. "She's smart," he said to Jase. "Are you still not used to the train?" he laughed as he looked at his companion who was turning a little green.

"Hey, I'm not used to this type of travel," Jase said in his defense. "Plus the cars are swaying."

"You should try to eat something."

"Not if I'm just going to throw it back up. Where is she?"

"I'm not sure. Kara was going to put her on a plane to Paris. She should meet up with us by the time we hit Berlin. I'm guessing maybe a layover on the way to Paris."

"Probably Madrid. That would be a common place to stop."

"I hope not. Santiago has eyes all over Spain and Portugal. If she called us from Madrid, he probably knows." He rubbed his temples. "She has to be more careful."

"She's only fifteen, Aaron. She's not a spy. You can't expect her to know everything."

"August has common sense. Stop defending her, Jase. I know you like her, but she has to take some responsibility."

Jase remained silent and stared out the windows at the German countryside. "Stay safe, August," he said softly. "I'm waiting for you."

~*O*~

Santiago Vicario had also heard the young girl's phone call to Aaron. He snapped his fingers and Ricardo, his business partner, came in. "Call Kurt," he ordered. "The girl is in Madrid now. She'll lead us to Steele. He has that inventor with him. I could use him for a new project I have in mind. Have him kill the girl and bring Steele and the inventor to me. I have some very interesting plans for them." He was smiling smugly.

"Yes, Santiago. I also found surveillance footage of Steele and Beckett in a train station in Germany. I'll send some men to intercept them."

"Excellent. Go ahead and do that. Tell Kurt not to kill the girl until she's with Steele. I want him to know he could have saved her before he dies."

Ricardo ran out of the room to call for the assassin. He laughed.

"Thank you, Miss Havens. I'll have Aaron Steele in my hands in only a matter of days."

# 7

*Paris Orly Airport*

I quietly strolled out of the airport with my suitcase. I hadn't seen anything suspicious on my last flight but I wasn't going to say I was out of danger yet. It wasn't worth risking it. I was on my way to the train station where I would get on my first train that would take me to Berlin. Hopefully I could find Aaron and Jase from there.

After that trip, I would travel to Zurich and Aaron would take me to the bank where my father had hidden the safe deposit box. Then I would finally know my parents' secrets and why the CIA was after me. It would be a great weight off my shoulders. I adjusted my bag on my shoulders and ran to call a cab.

"Gare d'le Est, *s'il vous plaît*," I told the cab driver.

"*Oui, mademoiselle!*"

As I rode through the streets of Paris, I tried to take in as much of the scenery as I could. *This will probably be the only time I'll see Paris, so I'd better enjoy it.* The taxi drove underneath the Arc de Triomphe and I had to smile. *If someone told me a week ago that I would be in Paris, I would have thought they were crazy. Now look*

72

*at me. I have been globetrotting around Europe and now I am going to Switzerland to find a secret.*

The taxi continued to drive through the city and I watched the landmarks pass by with wonder. "Is this your first trip to Paris, *mademoiselle?*" the taxi driver asked.

"Yes," I answered with a grin. "It's so beautiful. I can't believe I'm actually here."

"*Oui.* Are you staying very long?"

"No, I'll only be in Paris for a day or two."

"*Quelle honte!* What a shame!"

"Yes, it is." I gasped as I saw the Eiffel Tower in the distance. The driver noticed my interest.

"Would you like to see it? We're close. I usually like to show my American passengers. I won't charge you either since you're leaving the city so soon."

I was shocked at his kindness. "I wouldn't want to cause any trouble, sir."

"It's no trouble. Everyone needs to see the Eiffel Tower once." He began to drive in the direction of the large landmark.

As we got closer, I was in awe. How mere men could build something so beautiful and elegant was beyond me. I gazed at the architecture in wonder. "It's so pretty," I managed to say. "Thank you for letting me be able to see it."

"*Vous êtes les bienvenus, mademoiselle.* You are welcome."

I smiled as we drove away from the historic landmark. All too soon, we arrived at the train station. I thanked the cab driver for his gratuity and gave him a tip. Then I grabbed my suitcase and walked into the station to find my train.

The *Gare d'le Est* was a beautiful station. It was built out of white stone that glistened in the summer heat. The large entryway stunned me. It reminded me of Grand Central Station. The only difference here was the multitude of people speaking a foreign language. Luckily, most of the signs had some form of English on them. I followed them to a food court for dinner. My train ride would be an overnight one and they wouldn't be serving any meals until breakfast. So I needed to eat something before I boarded.

I found a small café and purchased a sandwich and a soda. I sat at a table and watched the people pass by. Every once in a while, I heard a sharp whistle from one of the departing trains. I kept an eye on my watch so I wouldn't be late. All too soon, it was almost eight o' clock. I tossed my trash in a bin and headed in the direction of my boarding platform. *Here we go again,* I thought. *Let's hope I can pull off another miracle. I'm so close.* So far Kara's identification had held up. I hoped it could get me to Switzerland without any trouble. I couldn't be caught when I was almost to my destination.

I stepped onto the train and handed my ticket to the conductor, who stamped it without any problems. "Compartment 14, Miss Fenwick," he said kindly.

"Thank you," I replied. I walked down the corridors until I finally came upon Compartment 14. I opened the door and went inside. It was simple, but mine. Kara had requested a single deluxe compartment. I had my own bed and a table and chairs, along with a bathroom. It was well-lit and cozy. I would be sleeping in this compartment overnight, so she wanted to make sure I would be comfortable.

I put my suitcase on the bed and got ready to unpack. The first things I looked for were my weapons. I found my hairdryer and broke it open. Various pieces of my handgun tumbled out. I laid them out on the sheets carefully. I would have to put my gun back together. Luckily my dad had insisted on showing me how to assemble a gun for some reason.

My ceramic knife was still concealed inside a bottle of conditioner. I wiped it off and put it down the top of my shoe. I found my ammo inside a bottle of lotion and managed to clean all the bullets. I sighed and let my hair down from its messy bun. I put the chopsticks aside and pulled my hair back into a tight ponytail to prevent hair falling into my face. As I observed the pieces of my pistol, I hoped I would be able to reassemble it.

It took me a while to remember my father's lessons, but I

eventually figured out how to assemble the gun. I held it up in the light and smiled at my handiwork. "You taught me well, Dad," I said aloud. "Thank you for teaching that obscure lesson. I never knew I would actually use it." I loaded my bullets in the gun just like Dad had shown me. *Could I actually shoot someone?* I thought. The memory of my bloodied father emerged from the fog. I gasped before regaining my composure. *I know that they had to be murdered. If I kill their murderer, then I could avenge them.*

I gingerly put the gun in my waistband. It could stay there until I really needed it. I looked out my window at the French countryside. "I'll be with you guys soon," I whispered. "Wait for me in Berlin. Please." I put my hand on the glass and closed my eyes in an attempt to wish the thought across the border to Aaron and Jase. *Wherever you are, I hope you're staying out of trouble.*

~*O*~

*Hanover, Germany*

"Keep moving, Jase!" Aaron yelled to his younger companion. They had been made on the train. He had noticed a group of men watching them while they had been eating dinner. He hadn't told Jase since he didn't want to seem on edge. Then he saw that they had guns. Aaron had kept his hand on his own firearm and ordered Jase to move.

They were almost to their compartment when the men jumped them. Aaron managed to kill two of them before getting Jase to the platform. They leapt off the train and walked to the nearest town, which was Hanover. Now they were stranded until the next train to Berlin.

"How did they find us?" Jase gasped as he leaned against a streetlamp to catch his breath.

"August probably tipped them off by making that phone call. I bet good money that those were Santiago's men. If they found us, she must not be far behind."

"Then we have to get to Berlin. We have to warn her!" Jase cried.

"They won't hurt her, at least not until they have me. I have to get you to a safe house. Santiago probably wants a new inventor by now. He wouldn't stop at taking you, too."

"I'm not leaving her," Jase replied forcefully. "She doesn't know what to do on her own. Plus the plan was for her to meet us in Berlin."

"Plans change. We have to get out of here. More men could be on their way. If we stay here, we'll be caught." He began walking away.

"No!" Jase disagreed. "You promised Conner that you would take care of his daughter, Aaron. You have a responsibility to keep her alive. If she dies, it's on your hands!"

Aaron stopped in his tracks and whirled to face him. "She got separated from us, Jase. Do you think that I don't think about that all the time? Santiago would have killed her if Kara hadn't found her. She would have died and no one would know. I blame myself every day for what happened to her under that madman. I was on my way to visit her family when that…accident happened. Maybe I could have stopped Conner from leaving. Maybe I could have saved their lives."

Jase was silent. "That doesn't mean that you give up on her now. We'll go to Berlin and find her. If we can get to her in time, then we'll head to Zurich. After you open her father's box, then you can do whatever you want. But we are going to find her."

"Then we're going to have to jump another train." Aaron began to walk towards the station they had just fled.

"Seriously?" Jase yelled after his friend.

~*O*~

*Somewhere in Germany*

I awoke from my nice sleep to a thump. My eyes flew open. "Hello?" I called. I checked my watch and saw that it was six thirty in the morning. *Who could possibly want me now?*

"Room service, Miss Fenwick."

I immediately reached for my pistol. My heart was pounding a hundred miles an hour. *The CIA? Santiago's men?* "Um, I didn't order room service. You have the wrong room." I stood up and went to stand beside the door. I quietly began to screw a silencer onto my pistol with shaky hands. I couldn't have the whole train waking up if I shot someone. As I tried to remain calm, one of my father's sayings came to me.

*"Don't put your finger on the trigger until you're ready to shoot. If it's there, you'd better be prepared to take down whatever's coming after you."*

"I'm ready, Dad," I whispered. I saw the knob begin to jiggle and I stifled a cry. The door was pushed open and came in front of me. I held my gun at the ready and tried to quiet my breathing. Through the crack, I saw a middle aged man come into my room. I remained absolutely silent and put my gun to the door. *If I can shoot through the door, I could sneak around him and run out of the room. I can find someone to help me.* My hand was trembling as I removed the safety and put my finger on the trigger. *Just breathe and shoot! You have to protect yourself!*

I quickly pulled the trigger and fired off a shot. I heard the man yell. Without any thinking, I grabbed my bag and prepared to run. I fled towards the hallway. I ran right smack into someone. I looked up and gasped when I saw who it was.

"Jase?" I cried.

He was also shocked. "August?"

Down the hallway, I heard another familiar voice. "Darn it August, you shot me!"

~*O*~

Fifteen minutes later, I was tending Aaron's wound. Luckily, I'd only grazed his shoulder. "I'm so sorry," I apologized for the tenth time.

"It's okay. You were scared and I didn't let you know who I was," Aaron said. Jase was sitting on my bed flipping through my book.

"How did you get on my train?" I asked. "I didn't see you earlier."

"We hopped onto it in Hanover," Jase explained. "It wasn't easy, and Aaron had to knock out the conductor. Luckily he had your compartment number on his clipboard. Aaron was going to get inside and make sure it was the right room. We had no idea that you had a gun."

"I told Kara not to give her one," Aaron muttered through gritted teeth.

"I thought you were the CIA or Santiago!" I shouted in my defense. "You should have said: 'August, it's Aaron. Let me in.'"

"Would you have believed me?" Aaron replied crossly.

"No."

"Exactly why I didn't say anything."

"So you expected to just waltz in and for me to stand there while you broke in?"

"I don't have to explain my methods to you, August. Just finish cleaning it."

"Fine." I put the alcohol soaked rag to the wound. I felt him flinch and he moaned. "Stop acting like a baby. Haven't you been shot before?"

"Yes, but that doesn't mean that it feels nice to have alcohol burning you!"

"You don't want it to get infected," I argued.

Jase was laughing at us. "Shut up, Jase," Aaron ordered.

"I've missed you guys," Jase answered with a grin.

I smiled too as I wrapped Aaron's shoulder with an ACE bandage. "I missed you, too, Jase. I'm not sure if I missed him yet or not."

"Hey, I wanted to leave you behind," Aaron joked. "Jase convinced me to come back for you. I guess shooting me was you repaying me the favor."

"I said I was sorry!" I laughed. Soon we were all chuckling about my skills with a gun.

"I have to admit it was a decent shot," Aaron put in. "Not many people can shoot through a door and hit someone."

"I'm surprised that I actually pulled the trigger," I managed to say. "But hey, I got my boys back," I said with a devious grin.

"We are not your boys," Aaron replied with a grimace.

"Yeah, we are," Jase disagreed while laughing. Soon all three of us were laughing at how ridiculous we were. All of a sudden, there was a knock at the door.

"Room service," a female voice called.

"Hide!" I hissed to Aaron and Jase. Jase dove underneath the bed while Aaron ran to the bathroom. I quickly pulled a robe on since I was only wearing a tank top and shorts. "Come in," I called to the worker. A young woman came in carrying a tray of various foods. I noticed she looked at the bullet hole in the door strangely, but shook her head and turned to me.

"Breakfast, Miss Fenwick," she said with a soft smile.

"Thank you," I answered as I took the tray from her.

"We will be stopping in Berlin in about an hour. Enjoy your meal." She then walked outside into the hallway. I closed the door behind her and locked it.

"It's clear," I said aloud. My two companions slid from their hiding places. "There's another thing to add to my list of crimes," I put in. "Hiding stowaways."

"It's not as bad as aiding and abetting a fugitive," Jase answered. "Well I guess they're kind of the same."

"You're doing well, August," Aaron countered. "Just keep doing what you're doing and we'll make it out of here alive."

"Well I'm going to go change. You guys can have my breakfast." I pointed to the meager meal. I pulled an outfit out of my suitcase along with my knife in a holster. Aaron saw it before I could hide it properly.

"Kara gave you a knife, too?" he asked in exasperation.

"How else do you expect me to protect myself?" I replied as I closed the bathroom door.

I heard him say something, but it was muffled by the door. I chose to ignore it and turned on the shower. At least I could clean myself for once. I had just finished washing my hair when I heard frantic knocking on the door. "Hang on a minute," I yelled. "I'm almost done." Just then, the door broke down and Aaron came rushing in.

"Get out!" he ordered.

"You get out, you sick pervert!" I screamed back while covering myself.

"There's a bomb!" he shouted. My eyes grew wide and my mouth dropped open.

"Shut your eyes," I said. He obliged and I grabbed the cloth robe and threw it on. "Okay, it's safe." Aaron practically threw me onto his shoulder and ran out of the room. Jase was in the hallway with my suitcase and bag.

"Go!" he commanded. We began to run towards the front of the train.

"What do you mean, there's a bomb?" I asked fearfully as I was jounced against Aaron's back.

"Someone stuck a device to the bottom of your breakfast tray. They were trying to kill you. Maybe get Jase and me out of the way in the process. Either way, we have to go." We were rushing past the dining car when all of a sudden the train shook. We looked behind us and saw smoke and flames coming from the last five cars. I knew the one with my compartment was already gone. "We have to uncouple the cars," Aaron said. "We don't want the flames to spread."

"Oh no, I killed people," I realized in horror. "This is because of me. I caused this." Aaron sat me on the ground and I collapsed to my knees. Jase put an arm around my shoulders as I began to sob.

"It wasn't your fault, August," he said softly.

"Yes it was," I cried. "If I had died in that car accident, I wouldn't be chased by the government. Santiago and his men wouldn't be trying to kill me. Those people back there wouldn't be dead. You would still be in New York and Aaron would be off doing whatever the heck Aaron does. It would be better if I was dead." I buried my head in my hands. I could feel people staring at me. I could understand why. My hair was wet and stringy from the shower, I was dressed in only a thin terry cloth robe, and I was sobbing like a crazy person. Plus I was pretty sure I smelled like smoke from the fiery crash behind us.

"August, don't you dare think like that. If you would have died, I never would have met you. I never would have known your smile, your laugh, or your sarcasm. I don't think I could have lasted much longer in that safe house alone. You pulled me out of there and into a real adventure. Yeah, those people were killed, but it was Santiago's fault, not yours. They're dead because he killed them with that bomb."

I looked up at him with tears streaming down my face. "Thank you."

He pulled me close. I didn't try to fight it. I was too much of a mess anyhow to come up with a snide remark. "It'll be okay," he whispered in my ear. "I'm going to keep you safe."

# 8

*Outside Berlin*

After the bomb went off, the train went into chaos. People were crying, so I wasn't the only one looking like a crazy person. Aaron had uncoupled the cars, so the flames were a distance from the dining car where we were currently hiding. I had gone into the bathroom and changed into a fresh set of clothes. As I buttoned up my mint green shirt, I brushed my brown hair out of my face.

"You are Lindsey Fenwick," I said to my reflection in the mirror. "August Havens does not exist. She is dead to you. When the police come, act like you don't know anything. You were on your way to the front of the train since your station was coming soon. You did not know about the bomb."

I quietly walked out of the bathroom and to the table where Aaron and Jase were sitting. "The police will be coming soon," Aaron said. "We have to be long gone by then."

"Why?" Jase asked.

"They're going to realize that the bomb went off in August-Lindsey's-compartment. They are either going to arrest her for being the bomber or take her away for more questioning. Either way, it won't be good once they start looking into her. They'll surely figure out the government wants her. Plus, they would probably love to bust two stowaways. Like I said, we have to be far away. We'll camp out in Berlin until the next train."

"That's more than twelve hours away," I put in. "What are we supposed to do for twelve hours?"

"We'll blend in," he answered. "We'll hide among all of the other American tourists sightseeing Berlin. They won't suspect us."

"Nice plan," Jase agreed. "We can tour the city and stay hidden. That's a pretty sweet deal."

I nodded. I wasn't a big fan of the idea. I just wanted to get to my father's box before the CIA realized that it existed and either destroyed it or took it away. But Aaron was in charge and I needed to do what he said. "Sounds good to me," I said with a forced smile.

Aaron noticed my demeanor. "We'll get to Zurich by tomorrow, August. You'll have Conner's box soon."

*If that box is gone by the time I get there, I'll shoot Aaron again. It is the only thing that can explain why all this madness is happening to me.*

We left the dining car and jumped off the platform between it and the other car. The train was stopped since they were waiting for the police to investigate. We began to walk towards the city. "How could they possibly smuggle a bomb onto the train?" I asked as we left the smoke and flames behind us.

"Santiago has friends in many places. He probably paid someone to plant the bomb onto your breakfast tray," Aaron responded.

"He'll stop at nothing to see you dead, huh?" I wondered. "Even if it means killing innocent lives?"

"I betrayed him, August. He doesn't like to leave *those* types of people alive. You escaped from his torture chambers. You're one of *those* people now, too. He won't stop until both you and I are dead or he finally dies."

"Joy," I muttered. "I have an insane arms dealer and the entire U.S. government after me. Yippee."

"It's fun, isn't it?" Jase asked with a laugh.

"How did you do this for two years?" I sighed.

"By listening to me," Aaron replied angrily. "You would be wise to do the same, August."

"I was kidnapped, Aaron. I already know it's my fault that Santiago found us. He *drugged* me and forced me to tell him where we were going. He was about to kill me, but Kara made it just in the nick of time. I'm lucky to be alive, and I do try to listen to you. Sometimes it doesn't work that way, though."

Aaron and Jase were both quiet. I knew they were processing what I had just told them. "I'm sorry I broke down the door while you were in the shower," Aaron answered. "But in my defense, there was a bomb attached to your box of rolls."

My lips turned slightly upward. "It's okay. If you hadn't have done that, I would be dead right now along with all of those other people."

"They're not going to stop, Aaron," Jase put in. "We'll have to be more careful."

"From now on, I'm not letting you two out of my sight." He put his arms around our shoulders. "We're staying together until we reach Zurich."

"What are we going to do from there?" I asked.

"I'm not sure yet."

For some reason, I had a feeling that as soon I got my father's box, I was on my own. It made sense. Aaron had to keep Jase alive. I wasn't as important: just a teenager who lost her parents and had to find some mysterious box. *If I get that box, I can figure out what to do next. Dad probably left some huge plan behind for me to follow. Maybe there's a safe house hidden away somewhere for me. I can change my name and create a new life for myself, one where Celia and Santiago can't find me.*

~\*O\*~

Once we reached the outskirts of the city, I felt relieved at last. "What tourist trap are we going to first?" I asked.

"I thought we could go see where the Wall stood," Aaron answered.

Jase and I nodded in agreement. We caught the metro which took us to a road. In the middle of it was a small row of bricks that led as far as the eye could see which split the road in half. "My family came from Germany," Jase admitted. "They managed to escape before the Wall was built. My mother was so happy when it finally came down."

I wanted to say I was sorry, but the words just couldn't come. I couldn't even imagine living in a divided city where you were kept away from the world. *I feel divided myself. I'm not the girl who lived a normal life in Philadelphia, but I'm not the type of girl who shoots people without thinking, either. I could have killed Aaron last night. If I had killed him, Jase and I would be screwed since neither of us knows how to survive on our own. I did manage to make it to Germany alive, but only with help from Kara. I sighed and rubbed my temples. If only I knew why I'm stuck in this nightmare.*

Aaron and Jase were examining the stones and hadn't noticed that I had slipped into my own thoughts. "It's hard to believe that this used to be a wall," I commented. I balanced on the row of stones while Jase was tracing the mortar between them.

"It feels so real," Jase said. "Just seeing it in person cements what my mother had told me. I wish she could see it with me."

I thought over Jase's story. *What happened to him? Why can't he see his family? Was he forced into service like Aaron?*

"We have to go," Aaron put in, which caused me to snap out of my trance. "We can't stand around. If we're being tracked, it won't be long until they catch up to us."

We walked away from the remnants of the Wall and caught a cab. "Where to next?" I asked.

Jase was looking up sights on his smartphone. "How about Checkpoint Charlie? It was an American checkpoint for diplomats and other bigshots. There's a museum about the Wall nearby, too."

"Sure," Aaron replied. He said something in German to the

driver, who nodded and began to drive away from the corner. "I haven't been to Berlin in a while," he admitted as he leaned back into his seat. "Last time I was here, I killed a corrupt diplomat who was planning on selling secrets. That was…nine years ago, I think. I never had time to sightsee, though. It was always fly somewhere, complete the mission, fly back to headquarters and get the next mission. Not a very interesting routine. It's nice to finally get to see a different side of the city."

I was a bit stunned by his casual revelation. *Thank goodness the CIA didn't get their hands on me. I couldn't bear to live like that, just killing people off because it was "orders." I would rather die than become a CIA agent.*

Before too long, we pulled up beside a small building with a gate. Aaron thanked the cab driver in German and we jumped out. I smiled when I saw the two men dressed as American soldiers standing by the gatehouse. "Mind if I get my picture taken?" I asked my companions with a grin.

"Go ahead," Aaron said. I strolled on over and asked the two men if I could take a picture. They happily obliged and Jase took a few pictures on his phone. Next I pulled Jase into the group and had Aaron take a few pictures.

"Aaron, come on over!" I urged. "We have to remember this trip as a family!" I knew he couldn't risk blowing a cover story, no matter how stupid the reason. That's why I had used it in the first place. Aaron reluctantly came to join Jase and me. I gave the phone to one of the soldiers, who took a photo of the three of us without any problem. When I got it back from him, I started laughing.

"What's so funny?" Jase wondered. I handed him the phone. Soon, he started laughing, too.

"What?" Aaron said gruffly. Jase showed him the photo. One of the soldiers had snuck up behind Aaron, who wasn't looking very cheerful in the picture. He had put up bunny ears on Aaron and made a goofy face. As Aaron was trying to figure out how to react to the humiliation of bunny ears, I noticed that Jase and I almost looked like a couple.

I hadn't realized it, but Jase had wrapped his arm around my waist and I had instinctively put my head against his shoulder. It looked like one of those couple pictures I had always seen on Facebook. *Could we be a couple?*

*No!* My internal monologue shouted. *If you two date, then you'll be compromised. You will never be able to be just friends again. You will be bound to him as his girlfriend. If one of you dies, it will kill the other. It would be best if you just stayed the way you are now.*

I smiled. "Screw you, conscience." I looked over at Aaron and Jase, who were joking around. "I think I can make this work."

~*O*~

We spent the rest of the afternoon touring the Holocaust Memorial and the Brandenburg Gate where President Ronald Reagan gave his famous speech. All too soon, it was time to get on the train and head on to Switzerland. "That was fun," Jase said as we got to the train station. "It was nice to forget our problems for a few hours."

"I agree," I replied. "It was a nice little break and a change of scenery." I noticed that Jase had put his arm around my shoulder again. I wasn't really sure how I felt about it. Fortunately, he realized what he did first.

"Sorry," he apologized. "There wasn't room for my other arm. Do you mind?"

"No, it's fine," I answered. I snuggled more into the crook of his arm so it didn't feel as awkward. I felt him relax into the seat.

"We're in two compartments," Aaron said. "Jase and I are going to be down the hall from you, August. Can you resist trying to shoot me if I come in to check on you?"

Jase laughed while I blushed. "Yeah," I replied. "As long as you announce that you're coming in instead of breaking down the door!"

"Fine. If you won't shoot me, I won't break down the door.

That sound all right to you?"

"Perfect," I answered with a grin. The cab pulled up to the curb beside the train station. Aaron paid him while Jase and I got our luggage. "I can't wait to finally get settled somewhere so I don't have to keep lugging this around," I groaned as I dragged my suitcase from the trunk. "I'm sick of carrying it."

"I can't, either," Jase agreed. "I can't believe this survived our jump from the train." He held up his battered laptop bag.

"Does it still work?" I asked in shock.

"Yeah. I made it myself. Think of it as an OtterBox for a laptop. I padded my bag and added a ton of protection. My laptop contains some of the government's best kept secrets. I'm not just going to keep it by itself in a bag!"

"Wow," I replied as I felt the bag. It was soft, but pretty heavy. "How do you not break your shoulder?"

"I'm working on making it lighter without compromising the level of protection. I want to make it waterproof, too. Hopefully I can either sell it to OtterBox someday or create my own company."

"It looks like it could be a weapon," I joked. "You could probably knock someone out with it."

"I haven't tried that yet," he mused. "Maybe that's how I should advertise it. 'Keep your laptop safe and keep thieves away!'" He said the last sentence in an announcer's voice. I laughed and gave the bag back to him.

We went into the station and soon found our train. I was sent ahead of Jase and Aaron so we wouldn't be connected. "Lindsey Fenwick," I told the conductor. He told me my compartment number and I went off to find it. My room was exactly the same as the one on the previous train, which is what I expected. I saw Aaron and Jase enter a room down the hallway and waved at them. I decided to hop in the shower since I still smelled like smoke from the crash. This time Aaron didn't try to interrupt.

I changed into a fresh t-shirt and shorts and sat down at my table to watch the sunset. I clutched onto a bottle of water left in my room and sat in silence as the sun's rays began to vanish over the horizon. *It's amazing how the sun is so dependable. It rises and sets every day without fail. Too bad life isn't that way. You never know how the day will be or in my case, if I will survive it. I don't know if I will be alive tomorrow or if Jase or Aaron will survive. Every day is a gift, and I will cherish it. But tomorrow I will be in Zurich and I will find my father's box. No one can stop me from finding out the truth about my parents' deaths.*

I stood from the table and went to lie down in my bed. Aaron and Jase hadn't come to see me yet, so I just decided to go to sleep. I put my knife under my pillow and my gun where I could grab it. *Aaron, you better not try to break into my room again,* I thought before I fell asleep.

~*O*~

*Somewhere in Germany*

I woke up to someone knocking on my door. "Go away," I moaned. "I'm sleeping."

"August, get up," an urgent voice called. "We have to get out of here."

"Aaron?" I asked. I pulled on a pair of jeans and boots, sticking the knife down the boot in the process. I put my gun in my waistband and went to answer the door. "Aaron, thanks for not breaking down the door like you did last time. I didn't want to have to pay for the damages…" I opened the door and gasped when I saw who it was.

There was a man with dark coal black hair and cold, angry blue eyes staring at me. His lips curled up into a creepy smile. "Hello, August," he said. "It's nice to finally meet you." I opened my mouth to scream for Aaron and Jase, but the man grabbed me and threw a hand over my mouth. He began to drag me down the hallway. "Now we don't want to disturb Steele," he answered. "I have plans for him later. I wasn't expecting him to be on the train with you to Berlin. Good thing

89

that bomb didn't kill you all."

I was fighting him, but his grip was too strong. I tried to grab my pistol, but he immediately caught onto what I was doing and disarmed me. I did manage to get his gloved hand off my mouth. "Let me guess," I said angrily. "You're an assassin, sent here by Santiago to kill me and Aaron and get Jase. You must be very high up in quality if Santiago sent for you and you're going to make it look like I died in an accident."

He laughed. "Smart girl. You see, Santiago doesn't like to leave witnesses behind who can snitch on him, even if they are pretty girls like you." He laughed evilly, which caused the blood to drain from my face.

*I'm going to die by an assassin at fifteen. No way out this time. I can't even say goodbye.*

We reached the back platform and he pushed me roughly against the railing. I grunted in pain as my hip made contact with the metal. "Such a pity," my killer stated. "A beautiful young girl slips on the ice on the back platform and falls into a ravine. They'll never be able to recover her body, either." He began to approach me and I closed my eyes in silence to prepare for the end.

"No," I whispered as frozen tears slid down my face. "Please, I haven't done anything wrong."

"Sometimes people don't die because of what they have done, August. Sometimes bad things just happen!" He reached to throw me over the railing, but I grabbed my knife and stabbed him in the shoulder. As he retreated, swearing at me the whole time, I threw open the door to the rest of the train and ran like I had never run before.

"Aaron!" I screamed as I fled. I knew the assassin would be recovering from my attack any moment. Jase came out of a compartment.

"August?" he asked with concern. "What's wrong?"

"Don't stop! Just go!" I gasped. I pushed him ahead of me and we began to flee together.

"What happened?" he yelled.

"The assassin who tried to kill us is on the train!" I cried. "He just tried to throw me off the back platform. We have to move!"

"What did you do?"

"I stabbed him," I whispered. "Where's Aaron?"

"He went to get something from the dining car, but I'm not sure. He's been gone for a long time."

"He's probably dead," I moaned. We reached the dining car, but there was no Aaron in sight.

"We have to find a place to hide," I said. "He'll be coming after us."

"Go to the front car," Jase said. "We'll get the engineer to let us in."

"How do you know he will?" I said as we rushed through another car.

"I can tell him that I'm an inspector," he explained. "It will buy us some time until Aaron can find us."

"Do you think he'll believe you?" I was trying to catch my breath.

"It's either this or die," he replied with determination. He pulled open the door and the engineer looked up at us with surprise. I noticed Jase had frozen.

"Sorry, but my boyfriend is feeling a little train sick," I said shyly. "We thought maybe he could hang out in here until he feels better." The engineer nodded his consent and turned back to the controls. "See, that wasn't so bad, right?" I told Jase.

"Nice save," he answered.

I stood by the door nervously. I didn't have any weapons and I was scared half to death. "If he comes in here, run," I commanded. "He wants me anyway. Jump off the train if you have to. Just get *out of here*, understand?"

"That's not going to happen. I'm not leaving you, August."

I sighed. "Stop with the chivalry, Jase. You're an important asset. He won't kill you. However, he won't even think twice about throwing me into a ravine or shooting me. If he gets in, run."

"All right," he replied reluctantly.

Just then, the door was thrown open and the assassin came in. He looked ticked and blood was trickling down his leather jacket from where I had stabbed him. He raised my knife and flung it towards me. I ducked just in time and the knife went into the engineer, who collapsed on top of the controls. The train began taking off at full speed. "Run, Jase!" I shrieked.

Instead of listening to me, Jase ran to the controls. "The train's going to derail. I have to do something."

I groaned and looked back at the assassin, who had a gun now. "You'll have to deal with me first," I said with determination as I stepped between him and Jase. I tried to appear brave, even though I was shaking.

He began to laugh. "Make it a challenge, *fraulein.*"

I dove right between his legs and ran towards the dining car. I stopped on the platform and saw a ladder leading towards the roof. "This is such a stupid idea," I muttered as I grabbed onto the rungs. I pulled myself onto the roof right as the assassin came out. As soon as I reached the top, I began to run for my life across the snow covered rooftops. *Of course it has to be snowing right now. It's Murphy's Law.*

A bullet rang out and I flattened myself onto the snow, which stung my exposed hands and face. "Steele is dumber than I thought," I heard the man say. "You're definitely not his protégé."

"Is that what they're calling me now?" I asked in an attempt to sound casual.

"That and 'the invisible...'" The blowing wind cut him off. I stood and took off again. I leapt over a gap between two cars, but my boot got caught on the edge of one of them. I landed with an unceremonious *thud* that made me dizzy. I cried out in pain. "Give up, August. In fact, why don't you just jump off? It will sure make my job a lot easier." I stood up, but fell again when I slipped on some ice. I heard a gun cock and I looked up to see the assassin standing over me with his pistol pointed to my heart. "End of the line, Miss Havens," he said with a laugh.

"Thanks for the chase."

I looked behind me and smiled at what I saw. "No. End of the line for you." I flattened myself onto the roof of the train right as it went through a tunnel. The assassin didn't duck in time, hit the brick wall, and flew towards the very ravine he had threatened to throw me into. I gasped and sat up once the train was outside the tunnel. "Oh, thank God," I said. "I'm alive." Then I remembered who I had left behind. "Oh my gosh, Jase!"

I climbed back down the ladder and found the control room again. Jase was sitting where the engineer had been. "I fixed it," he said. "It took some major work, but I managed to make it slow down." He then noticed my appearance. I was wet and shivering from the snow and my face and hands were covered with cuts from falling onto the roof. "You're wet," he observed with concern. "And you're bleeding. Are you okay? Where's the…"

"I took care of him," I said simply.

"Then he's…"

"I don't want to talk about it."

He nodded. "Of course. I won't push you. But if you do ever want to talk…"

"I don't," I interrupted harshly. "Now let's find Aaron. He's probably bleeding to death somewhere."

Jase decided not to push the issue, which made me relieved. He put the train in autopilot or something like that. "It won't go anywhere," he said. We left the room and went to find the missing member of our trio.

Surprisingly, Aaron found us before we found him. We ran across him in the hallway outside my compartment. He was holding a wet towel to the back of his head. "There you are," he greeted us. "I was getting worried. He snuck up behind me and hit me on the head. Probably was going to take care of me later after securing you two." He saw my bruised face. "What happened?"

"I took care of him," I repeated. Then I walked into my compartment and closed the door. I leaned against the wall and slid down to the floor. *I'm a killer,* I thought. *I let that man hit the tunnel with full knowledge that he would die. I'm a murderer.* Tears were sliding down my cheeks and I knew it was stupid that I was crying over the death of an assassin. *What if he had a wife and children? What if I just made a woman a widow? What have I done?* I leaned my head against my knees and quietly cried so Aaron and Jase didn't hear me. Unfortunately, I could hear them through the thin door.

"*Why is she so upset?*" I heard Jase ask.

"*That was her first kill, Jase. It tears you up inside as you run through all of the 'what ifs.' I felt the same way after mine during training. You eventually learn to keep it in a secret place inside of you. But the first one is always the one that haunts you.*"

"*Will she get better?*"

"*In time. She has to sort this out first. Don't push her, Jase. Let her work it out on her own.*" I heard someone walk away. I knew it was Aaron. Jase would most likely stand there until I was ready to come out. There was a knock.

"No, Jase," I said. "Go away. Please." There was the sound of footsteps walking towards Jase and Aaron's compartment. I curled up in a ball on the floor by my bed. My head began to pound from the stress of the past few days. I began to sob. "Make this nightmare go away," I pleaded. "I can't live like this much longer."

# 9

*Zurich, Switzerland*

I eventually cried myself to sleep on the floor of my compartment. Unfortunately, sleep didn't stop the nightmares from coming to haunt me. I woke up screaming from horrific scenarios most of the night. I wasn't sure how many times I would be able to take seeing my parents die or killing people. At nine o'clock the next morning, Jase woke me up and told me that our station was coming up. I calmly dressed, covered up the bruises and puffiness with foundation, and packed my things. Aaron found my gun and knife inside the control room and came gave them back to me.

"I don't want them," I answered as I zipped up my suitcase.

"You need them, August," Aaron argued firmly. "You have to be able to defend yourself. What if Santiago sends more men after us? What will you do?"

"I'll let you take care of them. I'll be a good little 'protégé.'"

"Where in the world did you hear that?"

I became silent. "Nowhere special."

"August, this is about the assassin, isn't it?"

"I'm not talking about that. I refuse."

"You have to talk to someone. You can't just let it eat at you until your humanity is gone. I know, it happened to me."

I sighed. "I killed a man."

"Good girl." He smiled and put my gun and knife on top of my suitcase. "Put these somewhere safe. I expect you to use them when needed." He then left the room to get Jase. I looked at the two weapons with distaste.

*You know he's right. Just suck it up and take them. You don't have to use them unless you absolutely need to.* I blew out a breath and stuck the gun in my waistband and the knife inside my boot. It still felt wrong, but I knew I needed to have them. I rolled my suitcase into the hallway and found Jase.

"Are you feeling any better?" he asked. I remained silent. "I guess not."

"Jase, please, just leave it be," I replied.

"No. Aaron even told me that you need to talk to someone. You almost *died*, August. You went through an extremely traumatic event. You killed a man, but even though it was self-defense, it still hurts. That trauma is ripping you up inside, but you don't want to admit it because you're afraid you'll seem weak. You are not weak. You are the strongest girl I know and I am positive you can get through this. I'm always here if you need to talk." He began to stroll down the hallway. I waited until he was far enough away before I allowed a tear to fall.

*He's one in a million.*

~\*O\*~

We took another taxi to our hotel where we would be staying while Aaron and I found the box. Jase would be staying inside and running surveillance when needed. Aaron had already laid out a map of the town on a table in the boys' room. "The bank is here," he said while pointing to a road. "We're going to go in this afternoon. August, you need to get that dye out of your hair. You have to be yourself again."

I was surprised and a little scared. *No more hiding. I'm going out in the open again.* "Okay," I answered.

"They're going to ask you some questions. They'll want to see your passport. You'll have to prove without a shadow of a doubt that you are the daughter of Conner and Lily Havens."

I smiled. "Can't they tell that I look just like my mother?"

Aaron laughed. "There's the August I know. Unfortunately it's not that simple. You'll have to go through a couple of different procedures. Luckily I had a friend clean out your record before we left the States. It should be just fine."

"All right. I can do whatever they want me to do. I just need that box." I went to the door. "I'm going to get my hair back to normal. See you all later." Jase waved absentmindedly from the computer. He had forgotten I was in the room after he realized the hotel offered free WiFi.

I walked into my room and went to take a shower. As I rubbed the color rinsing shampoo into my scalp, I saw the brown dye sliding onto the shower floor. I kept rubbing until all the dye was gone. I stepped out and grinned when I saw my normal honey blond hair streaming down my shoulders. "I'm back," I said happily.

I took out the contact lenses and revealed my dark brown eyes. For the first time in a long time, I looked like myself again. I changed into a khaki green button up and jeans before blow drying and styling my hair. Soon soft blond waves were curling around the collar of my shirt. I straightened my blouse, pulled my hair back into a high ponytail, and fixed my makeup.

As I walked back to Jase and Aaron's room, I began to feel my stress fading away. *I'm going to find out my parents' secret. I will know why the CIA is after me. I can figure out what to do from there.*

Jase opened the door before I could even knock. "I've been tracking Celia's whereabouts," he said. "She's in Vienna right now with another agent. Juliet is with them."

The color drained from my face. "Jules is alive?"

"Yeah, she's fine. Apparently she told the agent (his name's Regan) that you and Aaron were traveling to Vienna. They believed her."

I leaned against the doorframe to steady myself. "She lied, Jase. They are going to kill her when they find out." Jase took my arm and led me to a chair. I sat down shakily and tried to focus since the room was beginning to spin. Aaron crouched down beside me.

"She's alive. It's a start. We'll find her, August. I promise."

"You can't promise me that," I replied with an edge to my voice. "Admit it, Aaron. She's gone."

"They won't kill her until they're sure that she is of no more use to them. They'll keep her to try to get to you. To break you. They will squeeze every bit of information they can out of her. Juliet is alive. I will find her."

"She and Natalie are my only family," I said sadly. "Their mother died in childbirth and their father passed away from cancer before I was born. My grandparents were dead before I was born. Then my parents..." I trailed off to prevent myself from speaking about them. "If anything happens to my cousins, I don't know what I'll do."

"You won't be alone," Jase replied with conviction. He put a hand on top of mine. I looked up at him.

"Thanks," I managed to say.

"We have to go," Aaron put in. "Our appointment with the bank starts in thirty minutes. Come on, August. Jase, I want you hacked into the security cameras. If you see anything suspicious, notify me." He picked up a small box from the table. "Put one of these in your ear," he said to me.

I nodded and took a small earpiece from the box. I slipped it into my ear and heard a slight humming noise. *"Do you hear me?"* Jase said faintly.

"Yes," I said aloud.

*"You can whisper. The microphone picks up the smallest sounds. Just let me know what's happening every once in a while."*

"All right," I replied in a softer tone. I followed Aaron out the door and we went to the lobby. We grabbed yet another taxi and took off towards the bank. I sighed as we drove through the city. It was gorgeous and with Elizabethan charm, as if time had stopped. In other places though, it was very modern. We pulled up to a black granite building that read *Hyposwiss Private Bank* on the sign.

"This is it," Aaron told me. "Let's hope you'll find the answers you've been searching for."

We walked inside the bank and I was astonished by all the hustle and bustle. "How did my father manage to keep this account a secret?" I wondered.

*"It's really simple as long as you know the proper computer skills,"* Jase answered over the earpiece.

"My mother was a computer genius," I mused. "Companies from all over the U.S. would contact her for consultant jobs."

*"If she had the right training, she could erase any electronic trails connecting your family to the bank."*

"Maybe," I replied. *Could my mother be involved in this mystery, too?*

Aaron led me to a table where a tall bald man was waiting for us. He gave me a warm smile. "You must be August," he said. "I'm Klaus, the bank manager. You look exactly like your mother, except for your eyes." His gaze softened. "I'm so sorry about their passing, by the way."

"Thank you," I answered softly. "I inherited my father's eyes. I'm here to open his safe deposit box."

"May I see your passport?" he asked.

"Of course." I handed over my August Havens passport to him.

"Jase, make sure that the passport doesn't get flagged," Aaron murmured. "We can't get stopped now."

*"I'm already on it,"* I heard Jase respond. I grinned when I heard the sound of computer keys.

Klaus returned and gave me back my passport. "I have to take a blood sample," he explained. "Your father was very clear on what security procedures needed to be taken."

"I understand," I said. I hated needles, but I was willing to do whatever it took to get answers. I gave him my hand and he pricked my finger. I winced at the sharp pain. A few drops of my blood fell onto a strip of plastic. He handed a Band-Aid to me.

"I'll compare this to the samples of Conner and Lily's DNA," he said. "I'll be back."

*"Your father was serious about his secrets,"* Jase put in.

"You have no idea," I replied as I clutched my throbbing finger.

~*O*~

An hour later, Klaus was still asking me a whole list of questions. Even though the blood sample proved I was related to my parents, apparently it wasn't enough. "What was your first pet's name?" Klaus asked.

"We never had any pets," I answered tiredly. "My mom was allergic."

"Correct," he said. "That was the last question. You just have to do one more thing."

"What's that?" I wondered fearfully. *Cut off a toe? Hop on one foot? Recite my parents' Social Security numbers?*

"Your father requires the person who comes to retrieve the box to tell me the password."

"You've got to be kidding me," I groaned. *I'm going to kill you, Dad. Wait, someone already did that for me.*

"I'm afraid that I'm not. Did your father ever tell you a password?"

"No. He never told me the box existed until he died and Aaron told me," I replied while pointing to my companion who was almost asleep. I nudged him. "Aaron!"

"What? I'm awake!" he exclaimed. He looked around and realized with embarrassment that he was still at the bank.

"Did my father ever tell you the password to the safe deposit box?"

"No...wait, yes he gave me a clue. He said that the password was something that related to you. Maybe your birthday?"

"8, 14, 1997," I rattled off the numbers to my birthday.

"No, I'm afraid that's not it."

I sighed. "January 8, 1995," I tried my parents' anniversary.

"No."

I thought of my mother's nickname. "Angel?"

"No."

I tried his last words. "Be strong, August. You still have a lot of strength left in you?"

"No."

Fifteen minutes later, I was still rattling off various items. None of them worked. "Did your father ever call you a nickname?" Aaron suggested.

"Auggie," I said.

"No."

*"It would have to be more complex than that. Everyone calls you Auggie. What is something that only your father called you?"*

I blushed as I remembered one certain nickname. "It's stupid," I replied. "But my dad used to call me something whenever I was in a 'holier than thou' mood. It was usually around a certain week of the month." I sighed. "It's so dumb."

"Try it," Aaron urged.

I took a deep breath. "Caesar Augusta." Aaron started to snicker while Jase laughed out loud. "Shut up!" I ordered. "It was a stupid nickname."

"That's the password," Klaus said in relief. "The password was 'Caesar Augusta.'"

"Wait, seriously?" I asked. "The password was an idiotic nickname that my father made up when I was thirteen?"

"He wanted it to be something only you would know," Aaron responded.

Klaus looked at the large stack of papers on his desk. "Now that you've proven your identity, we can proceed with giving you the safe deposit box. Your father requested that you receive this first so you knew this was not a lie." He pulled a small black bag from his pocket. I took it and tugged the bag open. I was shocked when the object inside fell into my hand.

"I can't believe it," I gasped. "It's my mother's locket." The small oval shaped pendant in my hand was no ordinary locket. "It's been passed down through my family for generations. How did you get it?" I asked. "My mother never took it off. She said she was getting it cleaned…" I realized what had happened. *She knew she was going to die. She wanted me to have her locket. My mother was involved in this box somehow.*

Aaron was also coming to the same realization. He was muttering under his breath things that I couldn't understand. "I'm going to go get the box," Klaus announced. "Conner just wanted to make sure that you knew he was telling the truth. He sent that to me last week." He got up from the desk and left.

My hands were shaking as I held the locket to my chest. "I was supposed to get this on my sixteenth birthday," I explained. "The oldest daughter in each generation inherits it when she's sixteen and then passes it on to her daughter. This has been happening since my great-great-grandmother got the locket for a wedding present."

"That's pretty cool," Aaron replied.

*"Aaron!"* I heard Jase yell over the earpiece. *"We've got an emergency!"*

"What?" Aaron hissed.

*"There's a girl going towards the bank manager. She has a gun!"*

"No," I whispered in horror. I leapt over the railing that led to the vault and began to run to where I saw Klaus disappear.

"August!" Aaron yelled. "Stop!"

All of a sudden, I heard a gunshot. Everyone in the bank began to scream and run towards the front doors. I reached the hallway where the vault was and stopped dead in my tracks. A blond girl was standing over the bloodied body of Klaus. She was pulling my safe deposit box out of his fingers. *"No!"* I shrieked. The girl looked up and smiled at me. I gulped when I saw that she looked exactly like me. "That's mine," I said forcefully.

"I'm afraid that I am claiming it, August," she replied with a smirk. Then she took off. An alarm began to blare and flashing red lights lit up the hallway. I held my hands over my ears to keep myself from going deaf. I was beginning to rush after her when I felt someone grab my shoulder.

"We have to get out of here!" Aaron yelled in my ear. "The police will be coming soon! That girl looked just like you, August. They'll find some way to pin it on you."

"She took my box!" I screamed. "She took my father's box!" I tried to run away, but Aaron lifted me up by my waist and began to carry me back towards the front. "Aaron, no," I sobbed. "I can't lose that box."

"I'm so sorry, August," he answered with emotion in his voice. "But I have to do this for your safety."

*"What happened?"* Jase was shouting. *"I lost my feeds!"*

"Shut up, Jase!" Aaron exclaimed. "I can't focus right now!"

"Aaron, go back," I begged. "Please, we have to get the box!"

"We can't, August."

I began to punch and kick Aaron while screaming like a madwoman. "You jerk!" I screamed. "We have to go back!"

"August, calm down."

"No!" I shouted defiantly.

"Then I'm sorry." I felt a sharp prick of a needle enter my leg. The next thing I knew, everything faded to black.

~*O*~

*Vienna, Austria*

Celia Keene was extremely angry. She had been wasting the last two days in Vienna, but there had been no sign of Aaron Steele or August Havens. "Regan, I told you not to trust that girl," she told the agent roughly.

"I threatened her sister. She seemed genuine, ma'am."

"She would have said anything to save her sister, including lying. You needed to run a polygraph! This is an academy mistake. I could fire you right now!"

"I have a relationship with Miss Spencer," Regan said timidly. "I can get her to understand the gravity of the situation."

"Well threatening her sister didn't work. Let's try going through with our plans. I already have the sister in custody."

"You do?" He followed Celia to where Juliet was being kept. She was handcuffed to a chair and she appeared exhausted. Her long blond hair was matted and her clothes were mussed from being worn for a week straight. She was bleeding and bruised from various beatings she had received to try to get information about the fugitives' location. She looked up at Celia with contempt when they came in.

"Hello, Juliet," Celia greeted. "I know that you lied to Agent Regan about Aaron and August's location. I'm wasting my time right now when those fugitives are probably halfway around the world." She motioned to an agent to bring a laptop in the room. She set it on the table in front of Jules. Her eyes widened when she saw what was on the screen.

"Nat?" she asked hoarsely.

"Yes, Juliet. This is a live feed of your sister's cell in Washington D.C. So far, I have left her alone. But I am no longer feeling so generous." She dialed a number on her cell phone. "Miss Spencer is being difficult. Shoot the sister."

"No!" Jules screamed. "Nat! They're in Switzerland somewhere. I don't know what city, but they're in Switzerland!"

"I don't believe you. Kill the sister." On the screen, a man dressed in black came in the room. The digital Natalie looked up in fear at the man. He raised his gun and fired at the young woman. She collapsed onto the concrete floor in a fragile heap.

*"Natalie!"* Jules sobbed. *"No, not her! Dear Lord, not her!"* She turned to the director. "Why?" she cried desperately. "She was innocent! She didn't know anything!"

Celia and Regan left the room. The director had a big smile on her face. "You didn't have Natalie Spencer in custody," Regan said. "You have to have probable cause against her."

"Of course I didn't. I had to break Juliet somehow and her sister is her weakness. I set up an assassination with a body double yesterday and played it as a 'live feed.' I think we need to up the ante on our torture of Juliet. The beatings aren't working as well as I'd like. Start using electric shock."

"Yes, ma'am. I will." Regan ran off to get the equipment together.

"Director Keene!" A young agent came running down the hall towards her. "Director, we just received information about a shooting in Zurich. The victim told police the shooter was a young woman named August Havens."

Celia smiled evilly. "Excellent. Regan! Forget the electric shock. Prepare Miss Spencer for transport. We have to travel to Zurich immediately."

"*Yes, ma'am!*" Regan yelled from down the hallway.

# 10

*Zurich, Switzerland*

I opened my eyes slowly. Light was streaming through curtains into my room. *Wait, my room?* My vision came back into focus and I realized I was lying on my soft mattress in my hotel room. I remembered the disaster at the bank the afternoon before. *Aaron drugged me. I'm going to punch him later.* I attempted to stand up, but I was still dizzy from the after effects of the drug. I clutched onto my nightstand and forced myself to stand. I felt a smooth object under my hand. As I looked down, I noticed that it was my mother's locket. *He saved it for me. At least her locket wasn't in that box.*

I quietly put the locket around my neck and went to go stand out on my balcony. I looked out at the sunset over the skyline of Zurich. "Hey there," a voice said from the room beside me. I turned and saw Aaron standing on his balcony.

"You drugged me," I accused. "Why?"

"You were out of control, August. If I had left you be, you would have killed us both. I did what I had to do to keep us both alive."

"I lost the only thing that could possibly explain why everyone is after me. How did you expect me to act?"

106

"I'm sorry, but it was for the best."

"So what now, Aaron? Are we going to the tropics and hiding out?"

"I have a few safe houses in Asia that I was thinking about taking you and Jase to stay. We'll probably leave tomorrow morning. Kara can smuggle some new ID's to us."

I nodded. "Will you tell me why I'm so important now?"

Aaron blew out a breath. "It's a long story."

"I've got nothing but time," I replied as I leaned against the railing.

"Well...it starts with two people who were never meant to fall in love." All of a sudden, Aaron's room telephone rang. "I'll be right back." He went inside and answered the phone. *"Hello? Who is this? This is not Aaron Steele. You have the wrong number."* I saw his face turn white. *"August, get in here!"*

Without thinking, I took a running start and leapt over the railing of my balcony onto Aaron's. I landed and rushed into the room. "What is it?" I asked fearfully.

"It's for you." He handed the receiver to me.

My heart began to pound. "This is August Havens," I said calmly.

*"Hello, August. I believe that I have something that you want."*

I recognized the voice. "You have my box," I replied evenly. "I want it back."

The girl laughed. *"I am willing to give the box back to you. I have no use for it. However, it will cost you."*

I looked to Aaron and Jase who were monitoring the call. Aaron gave me a motion to keep going. "Okay, I'll bite. What do you want?" My hand was shaking and I tried to hold the receiver steady.

*"I want you to pay me $500,000 for the return of your belongings. You know, this stuff is pretty important. There are some interesting secrets hidden in these papers, all sorts of things about your dear parents."*

She was trying to get a rise out of me. I wasn't going to give her the satisfaction of making me mad. "Done," I answered. "When and where do you want the money?" Aaron and Jase

107

were making frantic hand motions to me and mouthing words. I put the phone to my shoulder. "What?" I mouthed angrily.

"We can't afford that!" Aaron hissed.

*"There's a gala tomorrow night on the other side of town. I want you to bring the money to me there. I'll be wearing an emerald green dress. I'll find you. You'll find tickets for both you and one of your companions in the hallway tomorrow morning. Yes, I know where your hotel is. Don't worry, I haven't told the CIA…yet. Tell Jason Beckett that he won't be able to trace this call. I'm smarter than I look. I'll see you soon, August."* The line went dead. I hung up and turned to my friends.

"Did you get anything out of it?" I asked hopefully.

"No," Jase replied in frustration. "I couldn't get a trace on it. It's like the call never existed."

I sighed. "We can get the money, right?"

"No, August!" Aaron shouted. "We cannot afford to waste that much money on a drop! We don't even know if that was the same girl!"

"It was," I answered. "I recognized the voice."

"It's not enough proof. I'll just go in without the money."

"Wait, 'I'll?' I have to go with you," I argued.

"No, you don't. I'll go in alone, incapacitate the girl, and get the box from her. It's simple."

"It's stupid," I countered. "She's after me, Aaron. If I don't show up, she'll be scared off. I have to go so she'll give me the box."

"It could be a CIA trap," Jase put in. "It wouldn't be safe for you to go to the gala."

"I don't care about safety," I replied. "I care about answers. Going to that gala and getting that box is the only way I can get those answers."

"If you aren't alive to get the truth, it really doesn't matter," Aaron said angrily. "You're not going and that's final."

I smiled. "You'll just have to drug me again. If you don't, I will follow you to the gala and mess up the entire operation. Would you rather that I know the whole plan instead?"

Aaron looked at me strangely. "Give Jase and me some

privacy, please." I complied and went to my room once more, this time using the hallway. I sat down on my bed and blew out a breath.

*I have to get that box back, no matter what. If I lose it, I could lose whatever secrets my parents were hiding forever. I will not let this journey be for nothing.* I quietly slipped out of my room and went towards the front desk. The concierge greeted me with a smile.

"How can I help you, Miss Fenwick?" he asked.

"Do you know where a good dress boutique is?" I asked. "I need to go buy a dress for a party tomorrow night."

"There is a Chanel nearby, miss. There are plenty of evening gowns there."

"Thank you." I turned towards the front door. *Chanel, huh? Well, that's going to be pricy. Good thing I have Aaron's debit card!* I held up the small piece of plastic I had pickpocketed. *Now to get a dress without getting caught.*

~*O*~

I found the Chanel boutique with little problem. As soon as I walked in the door, I was accosted by a saleswoman. She said something in her native language first. "I'm sorry, I don't understand," I answered. "I'm American."

"I apologize, miss," she answered.

"It's okay," I said with a smile. "You had no idea."

"What are you looking for?"

"I need an evening gown for a gala tomorrow."

The woman looked shocked. "Tomorrow night?"

"Yes. It was a last minute decision. Is that bad?"

"We'll just have to find a dress that will fit you without any alterations. Follow me…"

"Lindsey," I offered. "My name is Lindsey."

"All right, Lindsey. Don't worry, we will find a beautiful dress for you."

She was right. Soon I was dressed in an elegant gown fit for a queen. It was a wine-colored satin that complimented my complexion. Decorative beading covered the top of the very modest neck. The dress clung to my curves in all of the right places as well. The saleswoman retrieved a pair of gold heels that were high enough so the dress wouldn't need to be hemmed. She also found a pair of gold chandelier earrings. "You look beautiful," she proclaimed. "You'll have problems keeping the boys away from you!"

"Thank you so much," I replied in awe. "I'm ready to purchase."

She led me to the cash register and I tried not to look at the receipt. *Ouch. Aaron's going to kill me when he sees this.* I took the box containing my dress and the bag with my earrings and shoes. I said my goodbyes and took a cab back to the hotel.

I looked around the lobby and saw no sign of Aaron. I ran to the elevator and watched as it slowly ascended towards the fifth floor. *Please don't let Aaron catch me. Please let me be able to hide my dress before he sees it.* The elevator doors opened with a "ding" and I hurried towards my room. Unfortunately, I wasn't fast enough.

"Lindsey?" a voice called. I turned around and saw Aaron standing in front of me with his arms crossed. "What do you think you're doing? I've been looking everywhere for you. We're ready to go eat."

I clutched my dress box to my chest. "I went shopping," I explained, which wasn't a lie.

"For a dress," Aaron answered. "From Chanel, right? Jase keeps track of my finances. We know you used my card."

I pursed my lips, even though I was swearing over my bad luck internally. "I wanted to buy a dress," I said evenly. "It didn't cost that much."

"Five thousand dollars is your version of 'didn't cost that much?' We can't afford to spend that kind of money! Especially since I'm working around the clock to scrounge up money for the ransom of your box!"

My mouth dropped open. "You're going to get my box?"

"Yes. I don't want to, but I'm willing to do it so you can find out your parents' secrets." He sighed. "Show me the dress. We don't want to stand out too much."

I grinned. I had won *this* battle. If only I could figure out how to save Jules.

~*O*~

*En route to Zurich, Switzerland*

Jules looked out the airplane window at the Austrian landscape below. Celia had figured out where August and Aaron were and had immediately moved them all out of the Vienna base. Jules' injuries from the frequent beatings were starting to take a toll on her and she was feeling dizzy and weak. *August, run,* she begged. *Get out of Switzerland.*

Through various databases, the CIA had managed to trace the duo's path. They had escaped from federal custody while on a plane to Lisbon. From there, they had separated. It was here that they realized that Jason Beckett was with them. Celia had become extremely excited for reasons unknown to Jules. She had pieced together through rumors that the young man was an important asset who had slipped between the government's fingers two years ago. Apparently Aaron had helped him go underground. Now he was with both Aaron and August.

After being separated, the trio reunited on a train from Paris to Berlin. A bomb went off on the train in August's compartment. During the chaotic aftermath, all three vanished. They still weren't sure how they got to Zurich, but security cameras had caught Aaron and August at a bank trying to gain access to a safe deposit box under Conner Havens' name. As the bank manager went to get the box, he was shot by August, who escaped with the item. He managed to identify her as the shooter right before succumbing to his injuries. Now all of the CIA was searching for the elusive trio, who had hidden all traces of themselves after the bank incident.

Jules sighed. She also could not believe that August could

111

shoot and kill someone. *She's just a kid.* She wasn't sure how August would manage to escape from the CIA again if caught. At least she had stayed hidden for an entire week. *They won't show any mercy to her. She'll be lucky to survive the night.* She thought of Natalie, her sweet little sister, who was now dead because of her connection to Jules and August.

*I'm so sorry, Nat. If I knew what would happen to our family by running after August, I never would have followed her. I would have gotten us somewhere safe and we could hide from these monsters. But now you're dead and I'm being held captive. I wish I could have saved you.*

She was handcuffed to the chair in front of her. Jules wasn't sure how Celia expected her to escape a moving plane, but since August had done it; the director wasn't taking any chances. *What is she doing now? Is she safe? Does she know her father's secrets?* Jules never imagined her uncle as being someone the government would be after. He was a lawyer. Lily was a computer consultant. They both worked 9-5 and devoted their lives to their daughter.

There was one thing Jules couldn't put her finger on. Conner and his wife had been very secretive people. He didn't tell her and her sister that he was marrying Lily until he had already done it. He claimed that they had eloped so they wouldn't have to pay for a fancy wedding. They didn't know August existed until she was almost two. Conner wasn't living in Philadelphia at that time and he said that he and Lily had lost their address. She hadn't been so forgiving to her uncle for denying her the right to see her little cousin. Luckily, they moved to Philly and allowed her and Nat to see August whenever they wanted. *What if that nutty absentminded uncle of mine actually had a good reason for hiding all of those secrets? But why would he? Why would he hide his daughter from Nat and me? It's not like we would tell anyone.*

~*O*~

While at the hotel waiting, Aaron finished collecting the money. He had called a lot of favors and fortunately they had been willing to support his "cause." Jase was transferring money into our bank account and we would later cash it and bring it with us that night. My job was to stay out of the way and be quiet. Sadly, I wasn't great at following orders.

"So what are you doing?" I asked Aaron as he fiddled with a couple of gadgets.

"Setting up our equipment for tonight," he answered shortly.

"What kind of equipment?"

"I don't have to explain everything to you, August. Just stay out of the way. I'll let you know when I need you."

I sighed and went back to my room. I didn't really know what to do since I hadn't been assigned a job. *Aaron and Jase did work with the CIA,* a tiny voice reminded me. *They know what to do in this kind of situation.*

Aaron had told me that I was to be the "bait" in the mission. I would go in without a disguise and wait for the woman to find me. Once she did, Aaron would swoop in and capture her. Hopefully with some persuasion she would tell us where she hid the box. If not, Aaron said he would do whatever he had to in order to get the location. I just had to be in the right place at the right time.

I was still on edge about the girl looking like me. *Was that planned? Who is she working with? Santiago? The CIA? Some random organization I haven't encountered yet? How would she know about the box in the first place? Dad had only told Aaron about its existence. Maybe she found out somehow...*

"August?" It was Jase.

"Yeah?" I replied.

"Aaron's ready to brief us on the mission." I saw a sad look overtake his face. "I thought I was done with missions," he muttered under his breath.

I glanced at him with sympathy. *I dragged you into this mess.* We walked back to the boys' room where Aaron was waiting dressed in a tuxedo. "Wow," I commented. "You clean up nice."

"Thanks, August." He handed the earpiece box to me. I took

one and set it in my ear. "We're going to leave in an hour and a half. Your name is now Sarah Parker. My new name is Adam Parker. I'm your uncle." I nodded. "If this mission fails, I want you to run as fast and as far as you can. I'll leave Kara's number with Jase. Call her and she'll set you up with a new identity and a safe house. Remember that, August," he warned. "Your father wants you alive, not dead. Don't do anything stupid."

"I'm going to go change," I replied. As soon as I reached my room, I slipped off my clothes and pulled on my new gown. It still looked just as pretty as it had the day before. Then I began to curl my hair. While I twisted the strands of hair around the hot iron, I allowed myself to drift into my memory.

*"Listen to me, sweetheart. This was not an accident, understand?"*

*I was bleeding and my ankle was killing me. "What? What do you mean?"*

*"August, this was a..."* All of a sudden, the memory faded away into the deep recesses of my mind.

"No!" I cried. I hated the fact that my memories of that terrible night were so scattered. *What was the crash? Maybe someone put a hit out on my parents? No, that's stupid. Who would want to kill a lawyer and a computer consultant? Maybe one of my father's cases got messy.* "Yes," I breathed. "That's it! Dad must have got involved in a case that was way over his head. That would make much more sense. But why wouldn't I know..." I finished curling my hair and pulled it into an elaborate bun. I adjusted my dress and did my makeup. Finally, I threw on my shoes and assembled my weapons. Aaron had gotten a thigh holster for my pistol along with an ankle holster for three of my knives. I carefully put them on and went back to the other room.

As soon as Jase opened the door, his mouth dropped open. "August? You look beautiful," he managed to say.

"Thanks," I answered shyly. I came inside where Aaron was waiting.

"Are you ready?" he asked.

"As I'll ever be," I said with a smile.

"Let's go. The car's waiting for us." I took his arm and we

left.

"*I'll be monitoring everything,*" Jase explained. "*If I see even the littlest sign of something strange, I'll notify you.*"

"If *I* see anything, I'll abort the mission," Aaron told me. "No questions asked. Just get out of there as fast as possible."

I shook my head in agreement. "I understand."

Aaron had rented a limousine for the occasion and opened the door to let me inside. I slid in and then he took the seat beside me. We began to drive away and I smoothed my skirts nervously. *Just breathe. You are going to get the box and nothing will stop you.* I had no idea what would happen at that gala or even if I would survive it. All I could think about was learning my parents' secrets. *I will stop at nothing to find out the secret behind my parents' murders. They'll have to kill me before I'll quit.*

# *11*

*Zurich, Switzerland*

Still in chains, Jules sat patiently in a chair in Celia's hotel room. The director was planning Aaron, Jason, and August's capture with her team. "Jase and August are not to be harmed," she ordered. "They have value to me. Aaron, however...you can kill him."

Jules was horrified at how calmly Celia could order her men to kill. *I guess Aaron wasn't the bad guy. Why did I try to run?*

"Juliet?" Celia asked.

"Yes?" she replied meekly.

"You are to be a major part of this plan. I need you to talk your cousin into coming with you. We caught wind that she and Mr. Steele are attending a gala in town tonight."

"I won't help you," Jules said angrily. "You already killed my sister and I know you're going to kill me. Go ahead. I don't care."

"Oh really?" Celia pulled a photo from off the table. "Check the time stamp. Your sister is still very much alive."

Jules stared in shock. The photo was of her sister walking

through downtown Philly shopping. The time stamp was June 26, 2013, 3 o'clock in the afternoon. *That's this afternoon. But who did she kill in the video?*

"It was a body double." The director seemed to read her m___ ___ give up your cousin's location u___ ___ Thank you for pointing us in the ___ re sick! You let me think t___ ___ ays! What makes you think t___

___ister into custody. If you value ___. I will send you into the gala. ___ave with you without a fight. If ___ will be no need to hurt her. ___romise your sister's safety."

___against her bindings. "I will not ___our mercy!" she yelled.

___t just so you know, I will have ___ I know where she is and I will take ___ ___ you will save your sister and prevent August from further harm. She is in the hands of a madman, after all. Who knows what Aaron Steele could be doing to her right now?"

*Keeping her alive,* Jules thought. *Helping her find her father's safe deposit box.* "Fine," she said softly. "I'll do my best to convince August to leave peacefully. You should know that she won't go down without a fight. She's like her father in that regard."

Celia smiled. "Excellent," she replied.

~*O*~

I carefully walked down the hotel staircase towards the ballroom on Aaron's arm. "Are you ready for this?" I asked.

"Are you kidding? I've been looking forward to a mission for ages." He laughed. "The question is; are you prepared for what you're going to face?"

"I'm not sure," I answered. I looked down at my mother's locket that was gracing my chest. "But I'm about to find out."

We entered the ballroom where many couples were already dancing or enjoying a beverage of some form. I looked around in awe. "Don't look so slack-jawed," Aaron scolded. "You've lived like this your entire life, remember?"

"What is this party for again?" I wondered.

"It's the *Stadtpräsident,* or mayor's, birthday," Aaron explained. "All of the high-ups of Zurich are here to wish him well, including us."

"You can totally tell that we're Americans, though," I whispered.

*"Maybe you seem American, but Aaron won't,"* Jase put in. Aaron led me towards a white haired man wearing a tuxedo. The man smiled and greeted him. Aaron immediately began speaking rapidly to him in the native language.

"Wow," I said.

*"Aaron's been here before, August. He's a respected dignitary in Zurich. Well, at least Adam Parker is."*

"...and this is my niece, Miss Sarah Parker." I looked up and saw Aaron was introducing me to the mayor.

"It's a pleasure to meet you, sir," I answered as I took his hand.

"An American," the mayor observed. "A very beautiful one at that."

"Thank you," I said. "I get the looks from my mother."

"You have a very charming niece, Adam," the mayor laughed. "Do you mind if I steal her for a dance?"

I glanced over at Aaron with surprise. "Just go with it," he mouthed to me. "Of course, Roman," he said. "She's all yours."

Roman took my hand and led me to the center of the dance floor. I was scared half to death. I had never ballroom danced before, and I was afraid I would step on the mayor's foot and humiliate Aaron and me. "Do you know how to waltz, Miss Parker?" he wondered.

"Just from when I danced on my father's feet as a little girl,"

I answered honestly.

"Well it's pretty simple. Just follow my lead." He put his arm around my waist and I placed my hand on his shoulder. As we began to sway to the music, I looked around at the crowd lining the edge of the dance floor for a girl with blond hair and an emerald green dress. I knew technically she was supposed to find me, but I was still going to try. "You are a quick learner," Roman complimented.

"Thank you," I replied. I continued looking for the thief.

"*Stop looking around like that,*" Aaron ordered. "*You're going to expose us.*"

"*Do what he says, August,*" Jase agreed.

I sighed. I hated having them in my head. "Fine," I said softly. I turned back towards the mayor.

"How long are you going to be in Zurich?" he asked.

"As long as Uncle Adam says," I answered. "I think we'll be here until the end of the summer."

"Wonderful. My grandson really should meet you. I think you two would get along well." He began to lead me off the dance floor.

"Help!" I cried quietly into my microphone.

"*I'm on my way,*" Aaron replied. "*Just hold tight.*" We were almost out of the ballroom when Aaron came up behind us.

"I'll take my niece back," he told Roman. "I need to speak with her."

"Of course, Adam. She should meet Julien soon, though. I think they would be good friends."

"Maybe another time." Aaron pushed me gently back towards the crowd.

"Thanks for rescuing me," I said.

"No problem. He always tries to set his grandson up with one of the girls he comes across. Julien may become mayor someday and he wants him to have a proper wife."

I groaned. "Well he's not going to get me."

We stood by the appetizer table for a while, but no one approached. Aaron gave me the bag of money. "I'm going to go stand over here in case my presence is keeping her away," he told me. "If she comes, say something, okay? I'm not going to let you get hurt."

"All right," I answered. I stood patiently while Aaron went to the other side of the ballroom. It didn't take long to get a response.

*"Hello, August,"* a voice said over my earpiece. I was stunned.

"How did you get this feed?" I ordered. "This is a secure line."

*"I have friends. Plus the fact that I have your little boyfriend under my orders helps, too."*

*"Don't listen to her, August!"* I heard Jase yell. *"Just get out of there!"*

*"Silence him,"* the woman ordered. *"Now August, I have you right where I want you. Look up at the staircase. See the man with brown hair and a blue tie?"*

I glanced up and saw the man. He nodded at me. "I see him," I answered softly.

*"He currently has a gun pointed to Aaron Steele's head. If you don't want your companions killed, I would suggest that you follow my orders. Leave the ballroom."*

Almost automatically, I began walking towards the door that led to the gardens. "I'll do whatever you want. Just don't hurt them," I said to the mysterious woman.

*"That depends on your level of cooperation, August. Keep walking to the gardens."*

*"August, no!"* Jase shouted desperately. *"It's a trap!"*

"I'm heading there now," I replied. "I have the money."

*"Good girl. Stop by the fountain. I'll be there in a few minutes."*

I walked hesitantly towards the stone fountain of a fish squirting water into the sky. I sat on the edge and held the bag of money protectively to my chest. The chill from the marble slowly seeped into my dress. I shivered, but remained still. For all I knew, there was a sniper with his gun aimed at me somewhere.

"Aaron?" I whispered. "Aaron, abort. Get out of here. We've

been exposed. Just go, please." There was no response.

I heard footsteps come from behind me. "Hello," the familiar voice said. I turned around and saw the blond girl. She was wearing the green dress. "Do you have what I want?"

"It depends," I answered. "Do you have what I want?"

The girl sighed. She reached inside a bush and brought out my metal box. She set it on the ground between us. "Give me the money," she ordered. I took the black bag and pushed it towards her.

"Take it," I said. "Let me have my box."

She laughed. "Oh, August. You have no idea how to be a spy. I'm in control here. You do as I say. I have your friends. Right now I have a gun pointed to Jase's head in your hotel room. There's a sniper aimed at Aaron. You have to decide. Do you want your friends to live or your parents' precious secrets?" She lit a match. "It's your choice."

I watched the tiny flame in horror. "You wouldn't," I gasped.

"Try me. I already have all the important information out of the files. I have no more use for them. I can easily destroy them." She brought the match closer to the open box.

"Stop!" I begged. She stopped.

"I'll have your friends killed," she warned. I heard a slight pistol cock over my earpiece and shuddered.

*Jase...Aaron...could I honestly have them killed for a few secrets?* I opened my mouth to give my answer, but then I heard running footsteps.

"August, get down!" Aaron yelled. I turned around.

"Aaron?" I breathed in surprise. The girl grabbed me and put a gun to my head.

"Get back, Steele," she ordered. "I have strict instructions to bring her in, dead or alive."

"Well you'll have to disobey them." He had his gun pointed at her.

"How did you escape the sniper?" I gasped.

He looked confused. "What sniper?"

"You tricked me!" I yelled to my captor.

She laughed. "How else would I get you away from Steele? You have a weakness, August: your heart."

"August, just stay calm," Aaron said. "Don't let her get into your head."

"I have a gun to my head," I answered. "It's kind of hard not to let her."

"Listen, Steele," the girl said. "I'm going to walk out of here with the girl. In return, I'll leave your little scientist alone. But if you do anything stupid, I'll shoot her right here and now."

"You wouldn't dare," Aaron replied. "You know how valuable she is."

"Aaron…" I said calmly. "Let me go. You can save Jase."

He kept his gun trained on us. "That's not going to happen."

"You should listen to her," my captor said. "She's smarter than she appears."

Hoping that I could send a message, I locked my eyes with Aaron. "You let Jase know that I fought, okay? That I didn't die in vain?"

He understood the meaning. "I will."

I nodded. "Good." Then I jabbed my elbow into the girl's ribs. She cried out and doubled over. I took that moment to grab my gun from my leg and run back to Aaron. I pointed it at her as soon as I reached his side. She stood up and smirked at us.

"You think you've won?" she asked. "Just because you have guns pointed at me doesn't mean that you've won." Quick as a flash, she lit a match and threw it inside the box. Then she ran away through the gardens. Aaron raced after her while firing his gun.

*"No!"* I screamed as I ran to put the flames out. I dumped the papers onto the damp grass and attempted to stomp out the flames. I managed to salvage some, but most were damaged beyond repair. I collapsed to my knees beside the smoldering box. "No…" I sobbed as I looked at the ruined papers. *They're gone. My parents' secrets are gone.*

Aaron came back. "I lost her," he said angrily. He glanced

down at me and saw the hurt on my face. "But I have a feeling that you don't really care about that right now."

I sighed as I held the pieces of burnt paper in my hand. Tears were running down my face, but I made no effort to stop them. "This was my last chance to find out the truth," I managed to say while clutching the papers. "Now it's gone forever."

He looked at me sadly. "I'm so sorry, August."

"My parents were not killed in an accident," I choked. "I know that now. I know that they were murdered. But why? Why would someone want to kill them?" I turned to Aaron. "I know they were involved with the government somehow. Why else would you and the CIA show up?"

"August, I can tell you why you're special."

I just smiled through my tears. "I don't want to know. My father wanted me to find out the truth on my own, and I will do just that. I won't take the easy way out."

Aaron also smiled. "You sound just like your mother."

"Thank you. I appreciate the compliment." I looked down at the papers which were turning to dust from me clutching them so tightly. "I wish I could have heard the story from their point of view."

"Your parents were smart, August. You're just like them. I know you will find the truth." He squatted down by the metal box and rustled through the papers. I watched him reach inside and pull out something. "They did leave something behind for you. I recognize this." He handed over the thing he was holding. I gasped as I took it from him.

"This is my dad's .45. He used to shoot it all the time. Why is it here?" I peered at the gun in my hand. I rolled it over and found my initials engraved on the grip. Fresh tears began to fall.

"Probably for the same reason your mother's locket was left here. They wanted you to know they weren't lying. They knew you would need proof." He put a hand on my shoulder. I was shocked at the almost friendly gesture. "It's not safe here. We need to move." He took off his jacket and wrapped it around the still warm box. "We'll take this with us. Jase can analyze it and maybe some of the papers can be salvaged."

I nodded and stood up. "Let's go." We walked towards the car together. *Mom, Dad, I promise that I will find out the truth behind your deaths. I will figure out your secrets.*

When we got into the car, I kept looking at the box. "How did you know I was missing?" I asked.

"Jase figured it out first. He called me in a panic, screaming that he had lost your feed and couldn't see you on the security cameras. Then he managed to break in and realized that woman was hacking your earpiece. He tried to warn you, but you wouldn't listen."

"So he was safe?"

"Yeah. She never hurt him, August. She was only after you for some reason. I don't even know who she was associated with. She might be with Santiago, but I'm not sure."

I nodded. "We may never know," I answered.

~*O*~

Jules looked up in anguish as she watched her cousin and Aaron walk away. "They're going towards a car," she said over her microphone. "I couldn't get to them in time."

*"Good job, Juliet. I have a car waiting for you. You will follow them. Once you secure the location of Jason Beckett, try to win their trust. Say that you escaped. If you do well and convince August to leave with you, I'll keep your sister alive. Understand?"*

"Yes," Jules replied quietly. "I understand completely."

*"Great. Now go!"*

She reluctantly walked towards the awaiting car. "Follow that couple," she ordered the driver. He nodded and assisted her into the backseat. As the car took off after Aaron and August, Jules began to cry. *I'm so sorry, August, but I can't let my sister die. If I do this, at least you both will live.*

~*O*~

124

Aaron and I solemnly walked into their hotel room. Jase stood up from his laptop immediately and rushed over to us. "Are you okay?" he asked me with concern.

"Yeah, I'm fine," I answered. I knew my disheveled appearance told otherwise. "I don't want to talk about it." I walked past him and onto the balcony. I gripped the railing and looked out at the city skyline over the lake. It didn't seem quite as magical now. My father's gun seemed heavy in my hand. I traced my initials over and over again. *A.M.H., A.M.H., A.M.H... Why would you give me your gun, Dad? Did you know what would happen to you? Why would you mention teaching me how to shoot it? Were you warning me?*

My head began to pound again and I doubled over in an attempt to stop the pain. My memories were already retreating back into the deep recesses of my mind. *Too bad I didn't stay in the hospital long. Who knows how much brain damage I received in the accident?*

"August?" I glanced up and saw Jase standing in front of me. "Are you all right? Aaron told me what happened at the gala."

"I'm fine," I managed to say through the pain coursing through my skull.

"It's your head, isn't it?"

"Yeah. I get wicked headaches whenever I try to remember the accident. I don't know why."

He tilted his head in thought. "That wouldn't come from just a normal head injury. You may have been drugged, August."

"What?" I asked in shock. "Why?"

"You may have known something that someone doesn't want you to remember. At least, that's my working theory." He sighed. "You really worried me tonight."

"I thought they were going to kill you," I whispered.

"Even if they were, I would rather die than see you captured. Whoever that girl was, she's good with computers. She hacked your earpiece in nothing flat. I could only break communication twice before shutting it down altogether."

I looked out over the water again. "She said she would kill

you and Aaron if I didn't obey," I said absentmindedly.

"August..." I glanced up at him. All of a sudden, I knew what I wanted. What I had been wanting all along.

"Jase," I replied. He leaned in and kissed me gently. For a moment, I was in shock, but then I threw my arms around his neck and kissed him back. Not sure of what we had just done, we drew away from each other.

"I'm sorry," he said quickly. "I shouldn't have done that."

I put my finger on his lips and smiled. "Don't be." More in control of my actions, I kissed him softly and tenderly, until I heard a knock on the door. We separated and I drew my father's gun. I didn't know if it was loaded, but I could at least appear threatening. "Jase, get behind me," I ordered.

He stepped in front of me. "Not a chance."

I raised an eyebrow. "Who's armed?"

"You are," he said glumly.

"That's right. Now get back."

Jase reluctantly stood behind me and I slowly began to enter the room. Aaron was already at the door. He waved at us to be silent. "Go to your room," he told us. "Be absolutely quiet."

I nodded and pushed Jase back onto the balcony. I kept my gun pointed at the room while Jase climbed onto my balcony. I followed and we hurried into my room. The lights remained off and I sat down at the door we had just come through. "August," he said.

"Shh!" I commanded. "We can't let them know we're here."

"I just wanted to say that if we die in the next few minutes, I'm glad that I got to kiss you."

I smiled. "I am, too," I whispered. Just then, I heard a noise from Aaron's room. My demeanor turned serious again. *You have to protect Jase. If Aaron's dead, you're the only thing standing between him and certain death.* I silently took off my heels and crept onto the balcony.

"Be careful," I heard Jase warn.

*You are now bound to him. There's no way you can go back to being friends now.*

*Shut up, conscience,* I thought. I kept my gun held high and climbed back onto the other balcony. I cocked the pistol as quietly as I could. I was just about to put my finger on the trigger when I saw the person talking to Aaron. My mouth dropped open.

"Oh my gosh…" I breathed. "Jules?"

# *12*

*Zurich, Switzerland*

I was still stunned as I watched Aaron help Jules to a chair. She winced when she walked and her face was bruised despite her efforts to cover it with makeup. Her evening gown had sleeves, but I could see more bruises through the sheer fabric. "What happened to you?" I asked with horror. Jase had come back and he put his arm around my shoulder in comfort.

She cleared her throat. "I was knocked out right after I was captured. I woke up in an interrogation room in Langley, Virginia."

"They took you to headquarters?" Aaron put in.

"I guess that's what it was. I was held there for around three days. They began to mess with my head. They threatened to have Natalie brought in and tormented if I didn't tell them where you two were. Eventually I lied and said you were in Vienna. They took me with them and began to torture me again when they realized you weren't here. I admitted you were in

Switzerland but I didn't know what city. The bruises are where they tried to beat the truth from me."

I was horrified. "How did you get away?" I asked.

"The director, Celia, saw the story on the news about your incident at the bank. She brought me with them. One night, they took the handcuffs off and forgot to put them on before they went to sleep. Once they were out, I got up and ran as fast as I could. I started looking at hotels and I finally found yours."

"I'm just glad you're alive," I managed to say. "I thought you were dead."

"I almost was," she replied. Aaron meanwhile hadn't said a word. He appeared deep in thought.

"August, back away from her," he warned cautiously.

"Why?" I wondered in fear. "She's my cousin, Aaron."

"She's wearing an evening gown," Jase observed. "I saw you on the security cameras at the gala."

"They sent you in there to get August, right?" Aaron said furiously. "They probably told you I was the bad guy. Well the only way they're getting her is by killing me!"

"No!" Jules cried. "I escaped, I really did..."

"Shut up!" Aaron ordered. "Jase, scan her for bugs or wires."

"Jules, what did you do?" I cried furiously. "Are you working with them? Do you know what they've done?"

"I didn't do anything!" she screamed in frustration. "I got away! I got away!"

Jase grabbed a small device from his desk and began to scan Jules. It made a shrill noise once it passed her ear. Aaron angrily reached in and pulled out an earpiece. He smashed it under his shoe. "We have to move," he commanded. I nodded and went to grab my things.

"They're already on their way," Jules said sadly. "Celia's been standing by for conformation of Jase being with you."

My eyes grew wide and I turned to Aaron. "We don't have much time, but you need to do something for me."

"What?" he asked in exasperation.

"Take Jase and run," I said firmly. "He can't go back to that lab. I won't allow it. Get out of here with him. I'll draw them away."

"August, no," he replied.

"You have to do this," I answered. I slipped my father's gun into his hand and pulled out the other gun from its holster. "I'll hold them off as long as I can. Just go, please."

Aaron looked torn. "I can't let you go with them, August."

I smiled. "Who said anything about going with them?" He smiled back and took Jase by the arm.

"Pack your laptop. We're leaving."

"We can't just leave her behind!" Jase yelled. "They'll kill her!"

"We are. Now, go!"

"I have 'her' number," I told Aaron. "I'll call her when I'm home free. She can help me track you two down."

"Be safe, August," he said. He and Jase rushed out of the room.

"You like that inventor boy, don't you?" Jules asked.

"Yes," I answered. "That's why I'm willing to sacrifice myself for him." I cocked my gun. "You should get out of here, too."

"No," she said. "I've already made my bed. I have to live with the choices I've made. What are you going to do, anyway?"

"Escape," I replied with a grin. Just then, the door broke down and a swarm of agents came inside. They all had their guns pointed at me. I kept my own firearm pointed at them. "Let's do this," I whispered.

"Get down on the ground!" one of the agents shouted.

"Listen to them," Jules urged as she got down on her knees in surrender. I remained where I was with the hint of a grin on my lips.

I cracked my neck. "Oh boys, you don't know who you're dealing with." I slowly backed up towards the balcony. "You'll only be able to bring me to Celia in a body bag." I was against the railing at this point. I smiled cockily. "Catch me if you can, boys!" With that statement, I jumped from the balcony.

"*August, no!*" I heard Jules scream. As I plummeted towards the ground, I closed my eyes and clutched my mother's locket.

*I'm sorry, Aaron. I'm sorry, Jase. I'm sorry, Mom and Dad. I guess I wasn't strong enough to figure out your secrets.* Right as I was ready to hit the concrete, I was enveloped by water. My eyes flew open. *I'm in the pool! I'm alive!* My head was spinning from the hard landing into the water. I wasn't about to give up after this stroke of luck, though. I shook the wooziness from my brain and paddled towards the surface. As soon as I broke it, I got out and started to run. I didn't stop even when I heard agents yelling that they would shoot me if I didn't get down on the ground. *I don't care. A bullet would be quicker, anyway.*

I was almost to the lake when a heavy weight landed on my back and knocked me into the dewy grass. Handcuffs were strapped to my wrists and I was pulled to my feet roughly. I whirled around and was face to face with my captor. It was a man that I didn't know. He had brown hair and eyes and a cold smile. "Who are you?" I hissed.

"CIA Agent Regan," he answered. "It's nice to finally meet you, August. You're under arrest for escaping federal custody, resisting arrest, using a weapon without a permit..." I let him continue on. He was just a big showoff, anyway. He had caught me, the elusive August Havens, and he was pretty darn proud of it. As we walked back to the hotel, it began to pour and thunder and lightning roared overhead. "It looks like we'll be stuck here for a while," Regan commented.

I was formulating a plan and didn't answer. *Let's hope Miss Congeniality is accurate.* I smiled and hit his solar plexus. He yelled loudly. I quickly hit him in his instep and nose before finally whipping around and kicking him hard in the groin. As he was rolling around in pain, I took off running. The rain was making it hard to see, but I didn't care. I was free again. *Aaron, if you're around, you'd better stay away,* I demanded. I was running around the side of the hotel and hoping I could vanish into one of the alleys.

*"She's escaping!"* I heard Regan shout. I quickened my pace. All of a sudden, I saw agents rushing towards me. I screeched to a

halt and turned to run the opposite direction. Regan was coming with his gun pointed at my chest. I saw my last viable option, which was the lake. I sprinted towards the dark water. I wasn't sure what I would do once I reached it, but I was going to try.

I never learned what I would do at the lake because five agents tackled me. I started screaming like a wild animal. *"Aaron!"* I shrieked. *"Aaron, help!"* I kept screaming his name over and over again until they grew tired of my voice and finally sedated me. Before I blacked out, I managed to say one final thing.

"Jase..." I whimpered.

~*O*~

I awoke slowly. My head was pounding like never before. As I fought through the fog surrounding me, a phrase surfaced. *"If they know you exist, they will never let you go..."*

"Daddy?" I whispered. I moaned as a massive headache overtook me. I tried to move my hand to put it to my forehead, but it was stuck above my head. *What...* I opened my eyes and looked up. I was in my bed in the hotel room and my hands were handcuffed to the headboard. "You've got to be kidding me," I stated angrily as I attempted to break the chain.

"It's no use," a voice said. I glanced over and saw Jules handcuffed to a chair. "They use super strong chains. You can't break them."

I glared at her. "I don't want to talk to you right now."

"Too bad. I'm talking to you." She sighed. "August, do you know how stupid that was? You could have died!"

"Well if I had, I wouldn't be in this predicament," I answered while struggling against the handcuffs. "I would be halfway around the world by now. Maybe I'd be in Mexico. Mexico is nice this time of year." The metal bit into my wrists and I flinched.

"I told you. It's not worth struggling," Jules said glumly.

"We're stuck here until the storm is over."

"Is that why we aren't on a plane to Langley or wherever?" I asked while still trying to squirm out of my bonds.

"Yes, the storm grounded all air travel. We're stranded until it clears up." It was then that I noticed the howling wind outside our room. "Even if you could get out of those handcuffs, how do you think you'd escape? Celia, Regan, and seven other agents are guarding this room. They're hoping to draw out Aaron and Jason."

That thought terrified me. I couldn't allow Aaron and Jase to get caught because of me. "I'll break my thumbs," I said with determination. "I can get out that way. After that, I'll improvise." I wasn't looking forward to having to break my thumbs to escape, but I would do it to save my friends.

"How are you supposed to escape with two broken thumbs?" Jules gave me a strange look. "You're crazy."

Just then, the door opened and Regan came in. "Celia wants a word with you, August." He unfastened my cuffs from the headboard and helped me stand up. I almost tripped on the hem of the evening gown I was still wearing. He stuck his gun in my lower back. "If you ever try to get away again, I will shoot you," he said coldly. I just glared at him. He brought me into the living room and shoved me into a chair. Celia was sitting across from me.

"Hello again," she greeted. I remained silent. I wouldn't give her the satisfaction of seeing me broken. "So this is the girl who wasn't supposed to exist," she mused. "Honestly, I was expecting more from you. The daughter of Conner and Lily Havens, the invisible miracle. I guess the stories aren't true. Have you ever heard of Operation Lark, August?"

I shook my head no. I had never heard of anything like it. "Why is it important?" I asked quietly.

Celia laughed. "My dear girl, that, I'm afraid, is a secret. I just wondered if your parents had ever mentioned it."

"No, they never did," I answered with contempt. "I'm guessing it was for a good reason.

"They kept a lot of secrets from you, didn't they? I'm afraid that they were taken to the grave since your box was lost."

I knew she was trying to reel me in. *She'll try to get on my side and then convince me to join her to fight for "the greater good" or she'll threaten to kill Jules to win my compliancy. Either way, it won't turn out well for me.* I decided not to reply.

"You know August, I am recruiting you whether you like it or not. You will become a CIA agent. I won't take no for an answer."

I smiled. "Oh, Celia. You know that I'm more skilled than I appear. I will never join you. You can drag me to Langley, take away my family and friends, but you will never gain my participation."

The director smirked. "You will be amazed what I can do to you with the right amount of leverage."

"Try your best," I retorted with a steely gaze.

Celia turned to Regan. "I'm done with her for tonight. Take her back to the room. I'll save the hard questions for Langley."

"Yes, ma'am." He gripped my arm tightly and pushed me towards the bedroom. "Get on the bed," he ordered.

"Seriously?" I muttered as I got back on the bed. Regan handcuffed me to the headboard again and left Jules and me alone.

"What did she want?" Jules asked.

"She's just trying to get in my head," I answered. "I'm not letting her."

"August, I'm so sorry," Jules apologized. "It's my fault that they found you. They made me choose between you and Nat and my sister's all I have left. I couldn't lose her. I wouldn't be able to bear it if she died."

"Jules, it's fine," I soothed. "I can handle this. If anything, I'll get rid of the 'final piece.'"

"What do you mean?" she implored with confusion.

"Trust me," I replied. "You don't want to know." I stared up at the ceiling. *Dad, I may be the final piece of something bigger than me. I can't let Celia win. I hope you understand.* I sighed and closed my eyes. *Please, just show me a clue.*

~\*O\*~

I opened my eyes and found myself standing at the shooting range in Philly. "I'm dreaming," I said. There was a loud gunshot and I turned to see my father standing at a booth shooting his precious .45.

"Hey, Auggie," he greeted. "Go get the 9mm. I have to show you how to use it."

"This is a dream," I answered. "I can't shoot in a dream."

"You can do whatever you want," Dad said. "Just go get the gun." I sighed and picked up the 9mm from the next booth. "Line it up just like I showed you," he explained. I obeyed and lined up the three dots on the sights where I wanted them. "Take the safety off." I did carefully. "Now put your finger on the trigger and shoot." I slipped my finger on the trigger and shot the gun. It went neatly into the bullseye on the target. I smiled.

"Dad, why did you leave your gun at the bank?" I asked as I reloaded. "You would never get rid of that gun."

"Maybe I wanted you to have it," he replied. "But that's something you'll have to figure out on your own. I can't help you anymore."

"Why do you always say that?" I huffed. "Why didn't you ever tell me that you and Mom were involved with the government? Did one of your cases go wrong?"

He laughed. "Auggie, you're just like your mother. I can't tell you, though. You'll have to uncover that mystery yourself. Trust me, you wouldn't believe it if I told you." He looked at me oddly. "August?" he asked.

"What?" I replied.

His voice seemed to get farther away and the shooting range began to fade before my eyes. *"August!"* he called.

"I'm here, Dad!" I shouted to his disappearing figure. "Come back!"

*"August!"* the voice shouted.

My eyes shot open and I came face to face with Jase. I gasped and backed away. "No, no, no," I said. "You can't be here."

He grinned. "But I am. I'm here to bail you out."

"You have to leave, *now,*" I pleaded. "Celia doesn't know you're here yet. You have to get out of here before she sees you. I can't let you get caught because of me." I began to cry.

He wiped away my tears gently. "I'm not leaving you behind, August. I've lived that life. It's not any fun at all. I'm not going to let you live like that for me." He pulled out a lock pick and began to fiddle with my handcuff.

"Please, just leave," I tried to convince him. "Let me draw them away from you. You can escape and live a great life without me."

He looked down at me with determination. "I can't imagine living without you," he answered. The locks silently clicked as they released my wrists. "Come on, let's go. Aaron's freeing Jules as we speak. Regan moved her to the other room. Hopefully they don't wake up before they realize you're gone." He pulled me towards the balcony. There was a line attached to the railing that trailed to the ground. "Are you ready?" he asked with a smile.

"As I'll ever be," I replied reluctantly. Jase hooked himself into a harness and put my arms around his neck.

"Don't you dare let go," he ordered. I nodded, clutched my hands together, and wrapped my legs around his waist.

"I won't," I whispered. He stepped onto the railing and I sucked in a breath. *Please don't let me die tonight.* Jase slipped off the balcony and we began to slide down the line towards the street. I held onto him for dear life. We reached the bottom floor in no time and Jase pulled off the harness.

"Um, August, you can let go now," he said with amusement. I realized I was still clinging onto him.

"Sorry," I replied as I got down. The wet cobblestones were freezing under my bare feet and I shivered from the cold air that brushed over my exposed arms. Jase saw my trembling and placed his jacket around my shoulders. I looked up at the balcony impatiently. "What's taking them so long?" I wondered fearfully.

"I don't know, but it must not be good." A gunshot fired from up above. I clapped my hand to my mouth to keep from screaming.

*Did Aaron just get shot? Jules? What happened up there?* "We have to move," I ordered. "We can't get caught standing here." I pushed him into an alley and we looked up at the balcony for any movement.

"Please don't do that to me again, August."

"What?" I asked.

"Sacrificing yourself for me. I can't handle it, okay? I would rather die than watch you be captured and broken by those people."

"And I'm supposed to stand by while they throw you in a bunker to force you to make inventions for them?" I retorted angrily. "I won't do that, Jase. I won't stand by helplessly. I'm not a fragile china doll. I can take whatever they throw at me." For a minute, we stood staring at each other, waiting for one of us to back down. I wasn't going to give up. I cared too much about him to just let him kill himself. All of a sudden, he grabbed my face and kissed me. I did the same and wrapped my arms around his neck. His lips were soft, gentle, and caring. I meanwhile was attacking him with mine.

He ran his fingers through my hair and we were so close to having a make out session when we heard a thud. I pulled away quickly and we rushed into a doorway. He clutched me to his chest and I could hear his heartbeat through his shirt. "Jase," I whispered. He just held me tighter. I wished I had my gun, but it had been confiscated by Regan. *They won't let me go. I'm the girl who wasn't supposed to exist.* I closed my eyes and hoped for the best.

"What are you two doing?" My eyes snapped open. There were Aaron and Jules standing in front of the doorway shining a flashlight at us. "Come on! We have to get out of here." I grabbed Jase's hand and we began to run. I was berating myself the whole way.

*Why did you let that crush of Jase's manifest into a full blown relationship? You know that this will turn out badly for the both of you. You'll get captured and separated and spend the rest of your life aimlessly searching for the other.* I was pulled out of my thoughts when I saw that Jules was clutching her hand to her side. "Jules, you were shot," I gasped.

"It was just a stray bullet," Aaron explained. "Luckily, it just grazed her. I'll clean it up once we are safe."

I nodded and gripped Jase's hand tighter. *That could have easily killed Jules. Jase or I could have been shot escaping. Aaron could have been shot freeing Jules. We have to be more careful.* Aaron turned down a street and ran to the back door of a house. He banged on the door frantically. A tired looking, burly man answered and starting yelling at Aaron in Swiss. He grabbed him around the neck and started to shake him.

"Let him go!" I shrieked as I went to free him. Jase grabbed me and managed to hold me back.

"Sanctuary," Aaron managed to gasp. The man looked at him strangely. I caught the hint.

"Hey!" I yelled. The man looked at me and dropped Aaron. Jules ran to him and put his head in her lap. He walked up until he was standing right in front of me. "Didn't you hear him? We need sanctuary," I said crossly. He simply nodded and pointed to the house. Jase quickly led me inside with Aaron and Jules on our heels. The man followed and shut the door behind us. I blew out a breath in relief. *Another close escape.*

# *13*

*Zurich, Switzerland*

The man led us inside to the top floor of the ramshackle house. He spoke to Aaron quietly in Swiss before leaving the room. Aaron sighed and rubbed his temples. "He'll only shelter us tonight," he explained. "He doesn't want to associate with the girl who shot the bank manager for long. He does admire your spunk, though."

I managed to smile slightly. "Who is he?"

"His name's Rudolph."

Jase snorted. "Like the reindeer?"

Aaron frowned. "No, not like the reindeer. He's a former agent with the Swiss version of the CIA. He was one of my contacts when I was with the agency. His specialty is hiding people who don't want to be found."

"It sounds like we fit the bill," Jules groaned. Her face was shiny with sweat and her hand was covered with blood. I gasped at the sight of it.

"Jules!" I cried and rushed to her side. Aaron knelt beside her and gently supported her so she could stand.

"Let's take you downstairs," Aaron said with concern.

"I want to come with you," I said worriedly.

"It's better if you didn't see this. Jase, keep an eye on August." Jase nodded and Aaron helped her downstairs. I watched them with concern while Jase kept a firm hand on my shoulder so I didn't follow. He and I looked at each other.

"I've never seen that much blood before," I said numbly. "Will she be okay?"

"Aaron's taken care of gunshot wounds before. She'll be fine." He blew out a breath. "I never thought we would end up like this," Jase stated. "Hiding like common criminals."

"One week ago, if you would have told me that my parents would die and I would be forced to become a fugitive, I would have laughed in your face," I agreed. "But look where we are now." I brushed my hair behind my ears. "How did you end up a spy, Jase?"

He sighed. "I hoped you wouldn't ask."

"You don't have to tell me," I said gently. "I was just curious."

"No, we're technically dating now," he answered. "You need to know the truth about my past."

"Technically?" I asked with a grin.

"All right, then we'll make it official," he chuckled. "August Havens, will you do me the honor of becoming my girlfriend?" he implored with mock chivalry. It seemed so ridiculous that I roared with laughter.

"Yes, as long as you become my boyfriend," I replied with a smile.

"Now it's official," he laughed. He took my hand and I leaned into his shoulder. He rubbed small circles on my palm with his thumb. "Okay, well this is the story of a guy who became a CIA agent without even realizing it," he began. "I was a poor boy growing up in a small town in Iowa. I was an only child and my father had left my mother and me when I was five."

"That's awful," I said.

"It was okay. He was a drunk. Mom didn't want him around, anyway. As I grew up, I started loving technology. I was always taking apart things and putting them back together. I began to start thinking about making it my career. The problem was that my mother did not have enough money to afford college without scholarships. I wanted to go to MIT, so I started to enter inventing competitions. I began creating microchips that could do different things and entered them.

One day, I was standing at my booth after winning a competition and a man in a suit came up to me. He said, 'Son, have you ever thought about selling your inventions?' I told him I wasn't interested in selling them, just getting the scholarships. He said that he worked for the government and if I worked with them, they would pay for my tuition once my service was up. I agreed and found myself at Langley being forced to sign a contract saying I would serve them for five years. I was taken away without saying goodbye to my mother. She was told that I was killed in a car accident on my way home from the competition. I was never allowed to contact her again.

I began inventing a microchip that could guide missiles. I didn't want to do it, but the CIA forced me by threatening my mother. I completed it last year and I believe it's being sold for millions of dollars. While working, I hacked into the database. I discovered a bunch of secrets that could potentially bring the CIA to its knees. I securely downloaded them onto my laptop. However, they found out and were planning to kill me. That's when Aaron got me out. He had discovered the plot and couldn't let me die. That's how I ended up at the safe house in New York."

"Wow," I replied. "That's amazing."

"It wasn't so bad until people started trying to kill me," he joked. "So, August," he said. "That's an interesting name."

I laughed. "My parents wanted me to be unique," I explained. "I was born on August 14th, and they thought it was a good name. My mom's middle name was Maria, so they made my middle name Marie to follow her. My dad always joked that I was supposed to keep the tradition when I had kids."

"I like it," he said. "It's cool, just like you."

"I'm just glad I wasn't born in September," I answered with a smile.

"Yeah, that wouldn't be good," he responded as he laughed. We kept laughing and talking about our lives as the night drew on.

*Maybe it wasn't such a bad idea to be in a relationship,* I thought to myself as I smiled.

~*O*~

Jules tried not to cry as Aaron stitched up her bullet wound. "It's okay to cry," he said. "I know how bad this hurts."

"Why don't you say something to distract me?" she asked as she clutched the wooden table she was lying on.

He sighed. "Like what?"

"Tell me why you saved August," she replied off the top of her head.

"Her father asked me," he answered without expanding.

"Why did Conner ask you to save her? You were at the hospital so quickly. You knew ahead of time that Conner and Lily were going to die, didn't you?" she realized with shock.

"I'm not talking about this with you," he responded. "That's a secret that I will keep until August knows the truth."

She knew that she wasn't going to get any more information from him. She decided to try another subject. "Why was that man so angry with you?"

"I'm the reason why he is not an agent. He almost got one of my men killed and I called him out on it to the agency. He was reprimanded and removed from service. He told me the last time I saw him that he did not want to see my face again. That's why he tried to kill me today. Luckily, August stopped him."

"She's a brave one," Jules agreed. "That's what scares me.

One day she might stand up to someone who will shoot her rather than back down."

"She's already done that and won," Aaron said with just a hint of pride. "I didn't see it, but she stood her ground to save Jase from an assassin in Germany."

"August likes him," Jules stated. "I've seen the way she looks at him."

"He's head over heels for her," Aaron explained. "I can't even count how many times he's convinced me to go back for her. He won't leave her behind, even if it means getting caught himself." He gently prodded her wound as he finished stitching it. "There's an unspoken rule in the spy world," he stated. "Never fall in love. It will only get you killed."

"You speak as if you had experience," Jules said. She was trying to ignore how his smooth hands expertly examined and cleaned her wound.

"I have," he said.

"I'm guessing it ended badly?" she asked.

"She died," he replied. "I screwed up and they killed her."

"What happened?" Jules asked carefully.

He pulled out a diamond engagement ring on a chain from underneath his shirt. "Her name was Rachel Moore. She was my fiancée. I met her when I was undercover on an operation in Miami. She was a literature professor at a local college. We fell in love and continued to date after the op was over. I eventually proposed. Around this time, Jase got in trouble and I smuggled him to New York. I came back to Miami afterwards and acted as if nothing happened. Unfortunately, Celia found out." Aaron sighed and rubbed the ring between his fingers. "One night, Rachel didn't come home. She always insisted on walking home from campus by herself, even though I would offer to pick her up. I went to see if she had stayed late and forgot to tell me, but she wasn't in her office. I searched for her and found her in an alley half a block away from our house. She had been stabbed."

Jules shuddered. "Did the government kill her?"

"They never told me. Her purse was gone, so the police

called it a mugging. I knew it was a hit, though. It was awful the way they found her, all covered with garbage and dirt. I decided I couldn't risk staying at the agency any longer. I escaped and went to live off grid. I only came back when Conner and Lily died and August needed me."

"Why do you care so much about her? You don't even know her."

"She was my friend's daughter," he replied with conviction. "I owe it to him to keep her alive."

Jules was stunned. "I just don't understand why they want her."

"I don't think many do, me included," Aaron answered. "Only Celia knows the true secret of August."

"She's just a girl," Jules mused. "There's nothing special about her."

Aaron smirked. "That's where you're wrong." He began to examine the bruises on her arms and face. "You really took a beating," he commented.

"They were willing to do whatever it took," she said while wincing. "That meant beating me half to death to get what they wanted."

He didn't say anything, but instead applied a cold cloth to the bruises. "I'll get some ibuprofen for the pain," he said quietly. Aaron walked into the kitchen and conversed with Rudolph before coming back with a glass of water and a bottle of pills. "Take these," he ordered. She obligingly swallowed two and took a swig of water. "You never told them anything even after all of this?"

"No," she responded. "I wasn't about to let them lay a hand on my cousin. It wasn't until they threatened my sister that I revealed your true location."

"That's why you don't connect to people when you're an agent," Aaron said with an edge to his voice. "They'll use everyone you love as leverage."

"I already lost my parents," Jules replied. "Nat and her fiancé are my only family besides August."

"No boyfriend?" Aaron wondered. She noticed that he was fiddling with the engagement ring.

"No, I'm not dating anyone." She smiled. "Are you interested in my love life, Aaron Steele?"

"I just wanted to know if there was someone missing you back home," he answered quickly. "I might have to figure out a cover story if there was."

She shook her head. *Is he interested in me?* "I'm guessing you don't hate me anymore?"

He grinned. "Not anymore." He stood up from the table. "I'm going to go to bed. Are you coming?"

"Yeah." She stood and instantly stumbled. Aaron quickly scooped her up and carried her upstairs.

"We don't want you to pop one of your stitches," he explained.

"Of course," Jules replied. They climbed the stairs and found August and Jase tangled together, asleep. August had buried her face into Jase's chest and was clinging to his neck. Jase meanwhile had wrapped his arms around her back and was holding her close to him as if he was afraid she would slip away sometime in the night.

"I shouldn't have let this happen," Aaron sighed. "Love makes you weak." He went to go lie down in another corner of the room. Jules leaned down and kissed August on the cheek before lying down as well. She wasn't sure if she agreed with Aaron, but she thought they were cute.

"Just don't become Romeo and Juliet, kids," she whispered as she lay down. She allowed a small smile as she had been named after the famous literary character. *Hopefully my future won't be as tragic as hers.* She closed her eyes and allowed herself to fall into a deep sleep.

~*O*~

*Bang! Bang! Bang!* The noise woke us up at once. Jase was startled also and we bumped heads. "Ow," I groaned as I rubbed the spot we had hit.

"Sorry," he apologized.

"Get up!" Aaron hissed. "We have to hide."

"Where?" I asked while looking around the bare room.

Aaron rushed over to the far wall and pressed on a panel. The wall swung open to reveal a hidden room. "Go," he said. Jase pulled me inside and Jules came in behind us. Aaron grabbed our belongings and threw them in before carefully shutting the door and latching it. We were now stuck inside a tiny room which smelled of old socks. I plugged my nose to keep from gagging. Jase had his arms around me and I didn't try to get them off. Aaron had his gun at the ready and Jules had her eyes closed. I had a fleeting thought that this must be how the Jews felt during Hitler's rule. My heart began to pound rapidly.

I could hear Rudolph yelling at the men downstairs. *Please keep them away*, I begged. *Don't let them find us.*

"If anything happens, run," Aaron whispered. "Try to get away if you can." We all nodded and held our breath in hopes that we wouldn't be heard. Footsteps began to come up the stairs.

*"Search the place,"* a voice said. *"Leave nothing unturned."* It was Regan. My blood ran cold. A memory exploded into full blown color in the back of my mind.

*I'm running down a dark alley. There are men chasing me. I don't know why, but it seems like they're after me. My swollen ankle is slowing me down tremendously and I'm crying from the immense pain.*

*"Stop, August! We're not here to hurt you!" a voice calls through the darkness.*

Go away, *I beg.* Please, just go away. *Suddenly, I smack right into something. The scene begins to fade.*

I gasped and pulled myself out of my thoughts. My head was erupting in agony and I whimpered softly. Jase clutched a hand over my mouth. I could hear the men right beyond the wall.

*"Did you hear that?"* Regan asked. *"Everyone stay still for a minute."* I saw Jules' eyes go wide as she held onto Aaron's hand.

I tried to ignore the horrible pain pulsing behind my eyes.

*Stop, please, just stop,* I pleaded to my headache. *I won't try to remember anymore.* Unfortunately, the migraine didn't believe me and was pounding even more. I had tears streaming down my face and wetting Jase's hand.

*"I don't hear anything, boss,"* one of the men said. *"I don't think they're here."*

*"They have to be here. Rudolph probably threw us off the trail. We'll come back with the dogs."* Their footsteps seemed to grow farther away. We heard the door slam, but Aaron waited a few minutes before allowing us to leave the hiding place. "Hurry," he urged. I almost doubled over from the pain in my head. Jase supported me.

"Is it one of your headaches?" he wondered in concern.

"Yes," I managed to say. "It's killing me." He didn't reply, but instead picked me up and carried me down the stairs to the kitchen. My lip was bleeding from me biting it so I wouldn't scream. Aaron said a few words to Rudolph, who pointed in another direction.

"Follow me," Aaron told us. We went out the door and ran down the tight streets. I was being jounced against Jase's chest, but I didn't care. I closed my eyes and let the pain carry me away.

"August, stay awake," I heard Jase say.

"I can't," I whispered faintly. I gave myself up to the blackness and began to fall down a deep dark hole.

~\*O\*~

I woke up to a swaying feeling. I opened my eyes and saw that we were on a subway train. My head was in Jase's lap and he was stroking my hair. Aaron and Jules were sitting across the aisle. "Where are we?" I moaned.

Jase jumped. "You're awake!" he said with surprise.

"Yeah, I'm awake. Did you think I died or something?"

"No…we're en route to another safe house in Zurich.

Aaron's going to get in contact with Kara and request new identities for all of us. Then we'll take a train out of Europe and escape to Asia. We'll stay there until the heat dies down."

I nodded. The pain in my head was mostly gone, but it still ached slightly. "I don't understand why I hurt so badly," I managed to say as I closed my eyes.

"It's called a memory block," Aaron said. "The CIA uses it sometimes. It blocks your memories so you don't remember what they don't want you to know. It's a fairly new drug. They've started using it on people they interrogate. I never agreed with the practice, which is partly why I left."

"Why would they block August's memories?" Jules asked with concern. "She doesn't know anything dangerous."

"Maybe she does and the agency doesn't want her to know the truth. They want to entice her with her parents' secrets in order to recruit her. She was found three blocks away from the accident scene. She got away somehow. August may have found something that she can't know and they want her to come willingly."

"I get wicked headaches when I try to remember. I can see some parts of that night, but it quickly fades when my head starts hurting," I put in.

"That's one of the side effects," Jase explained. "I helped invent that drug. It targets the memory and prevents it from surfacing by using those headaches to discourage the victim from remembering. I think they were working on reducing the headache part when I left."

"You helped invent this thing?" I questioned painfully.

"I was forced to. They wanted me on the team for some odd reason. I came up with the navigation part of the drug. The others invented the blocking and headache."

"Whatever it is, it sucks," I replied. "Can it be overridden?"

"If the user is persistent enough, I think it can. You have to overcome the pain, August. Don't allow it to take over because it will knock you out again. That's the worst case scenario part of the drug. If it can't discourage you through pain, it will simply knock you out so you can't try to remember. You have to be sneaky."

I smiled a little. "I can do that."

He kissed my forehead. "I know you can. You're stronger than them. You can defeat their memory block. It will just take time, okay?"

I nodded. "Okay." The train began to slow down. Aaron stood up.

"This is our stop. Let's go." Jase helped me stand and we hurried off the train and into the station. We melted into the crowd and traveled up the stairs into the main part of the city. Aaron approached a fancy apartment building. "This way."

We followed him and quietly climbed up the steps to the third floor. Aaron stopped by one of the doors and slid a key in the lock. It opened and we piled in the apartment. "Wow," I said in awe. "This is gorgeous." The first thing I saw was a large breakfast bar with a white chandelier hanging over it. Everything was painted in a pure airy white. Aaron rushed to another room while Jase, Jules, and I just stared at the apartment in wonder.

"Is this a CIA safe house?" I asked as I sat down on one of the bar stools.

"Probably," Jase answered. "That might be why we didn't go here in the first place."

I swung in the seat. "Are we safe to stay here?"

"Not for very long. Regan will most likely latch onto this as an option soon. Aaron's just using it to find Kara."

"Jase, get in here!" Aaron yelled. "I need you to make a secure line!"

"On it!" Jase hurried into the other room. Jules collapsed onto one of the plush couches in the living room.

"I could get used to this side of the spy life," she sighed as she snuggled into the pillows.

"I could, too," I laughed. "Getting dressed up fancy is also a plus."

"I've forgotten what it feels like to laugh," Jules said. "Isn't that sad?"

"It is," I agreed. "But I feel the same way."

"August, be honest with me," Jules said seriously. I walked into the living room and plopped down on the other side of the couch.

"Yeah?" I asked softly.

"Did you kill that bank manager? It was all over the news."

I knew that question was coming, but I still wasn't excited about answering it. "No, I did not kill him. I have a look alike. I don't know who she is, but she posed as me and shot Klaus, the bank manager. She stole my box and ran off. I tried to get it back from her, but she burned the papers inside. I don't know what happened to it after the night we all reunited."

Jules was silent and I knew she was thinking. "Why would she frame you for a murder you didn't commit?"

"I don't know," I replied. "All I know is that I didn't do it. That's all that matters." I could hear Aaron and Jase pounding away at keyboards in the other room. "I hope they know what they're doing."

"I do, too," Jules said. "We can't be caught after all we've been through."

I stared up at the ceiling. "I just wish I could remember what happened to me that night. I think Dad told me to run, but I'm not for sure. I can't think about it without getting a migraine, though."

"You can beat it, August. You are smart just like your mom. You'll figure it out."

I smiled. "I hope that it won't get me killed in the process."

# 14

*Zurich, Switzerland*

After two hours of impatient waiting, Aaron finally came into the living room. "I established contact with Kara," he said with a smile. "She's sending us new passports right now. I can print and assemble them right here."

"Anything we need to know about our new identities?" I asked.

"You and Jase are going to be boyfriend and girlfriend. Jules and I are married." I saw him take a ring hanging on a chain from underneath his shirt. "I already have the ring."

"Where did you..."

"It's a long story," Jules cut in. She allowed Aaron to slip the ring on her finger. There was a strange look on her face that I couldn't read. I decided to drop the subject. I was perfectly content with my new identity. Jase and I were already together anyway. It wasn't a lie. I just hoped my background wasn't complicated.

I could hear Jase's words in my head. *"You get used to it after a while. I can slip on a new identity like a glove."* Sadly, I was becoming that way, too. *Welcome to my new reality.*

There was a big closet in the bedroom that contained clothes of all sizes. I took the opportunity to change out of my torn dress and into a new outfit. I pulled on jeans, a blue and red plaid shirt, and a black leather jacket. I finished my ensemble with a pair of black boots and putting my hair in a side ponytail. I put on a layer of bright red lipstick and went into the living room again. "Wow," Jules exclaimed. "You look great."

"There are all sorts of clothes in there," I said. "Feel free to go put something on." She walked into the bedroom and shut the door. I went to the office where Aaron and Jase were working on our passports. "How's it going?" I asked as I leaned on the door frame and watched them.

"Fine," Aaron answered absentmindedly.

"When are we leaving?"

"This evening," Jase replied. "Kara already sent tickets."

"Train, plane, or bus?"

"It's a train for now until we get out of the country. Then we'll take a plane to Japan where Aaron has a safe house."

"Very cool," I commented. "What happened to my box?"

"It's with Kara," Aaron said. "I sent it to her to keep it safe when you and Jules were captured. Once we're settled, I'll have her send it back to us." He caught the look I was giving him. "August, I promise that she won't do anything to it. It's in a safe in her apartment in Lisbon."

I huffed. "Fine. But I want that box in my hands when we reach Japan. Maybe we can salvage some of the papers."

"Okay," Aaron replied. "Now let us get some work done, all right?"

I let them be and went back to the living room. Jules had changed and was flipping through a magazine. "Are they almost ready?" she wondered.

"No, they're still putting together passports," I answered. "We leave on a train this evening."

"Good," she mused. "Aaron mentioned that we were going

to Asia. I can't wait to get settled. This whole running for my life thing is getting old."

"I agree," I said with a laugh. "It will be a nice vacation."

"Please don't tell me that you're starting to consider this normal," Jules pleaded.

"I don't think our lives will ever be normal again," I answered slyly. "But we can always dream, right?"

"I guess," Jules replied with exasperation.

Aaron came in at that moment. "The passports are ready. I'm ready to brief you guys." We went into the office where four sets of identification and tickets were waiting on the desk. "We're taking a train to Prague this evening," he explained. "From there, we'll fly towards Japan. It will take a while, so we need to have our cover stories established. Jase, you are Charles Fowler. August, you are his girlfriend Marie Howard. You're traveling together to your uncle's house in Prague. Go in the other room and figure out your background. Jules and I will come up with ours in here."

We followed orders and walked into the other room. "So..." I started. "What's our story?"

"Let's say we've been dating for two years," Jase said. "I don't think your parents would let you head off with a boy you've just met."

"Perfect," I said. "Where could we meet? We're like three years apart."

"You're fifteen."

"I'll be sixteen in less than two months, Einstein," I replied sarcastically. "When is your birthday?"

"It was last month. I just turned nineteen."

"Cradle robber," I joked.

"Hey, you said yes," he replied with a smirk. "How about we met at the coffee shop in town? I saw you, you saw me. I sat down and we started talking. I asked you out on a date and you accepted. We've been together ever since."

"I like it," I smiled. "We need to know more about each other. If we're asked, we need to know crucial things."

"This feels like *The Proposal*," Jase laughed. "All right, what's your favorite food?"

"That would be chicken and noodles," I said. "My mom made the best."

He grinned. "My mom did, too. I like steak, personally."

"Well you're an expensive date," I laughed.

"I'm not afraid to admit it, either. My favorite movie's *Back to the Future*. What's yours?"

"I love *Mission: Impossible*," I said with a smile. "My dad raised me on action movies."

"Nice," he commented. "I could see Aaron being on a team like that."

I snickered. "I could, too."

We bounced around and told our favorite hobbies, books, and even ice cream. I told some stories of my childhood, and he did the same. We laughed until our stomachs hurt and all too soon Aaron and Jules were coming back in the living room.

"Are you ready?" Aaron asked.

"As we'll ever be," I answered with a smile.

"Good. We're leaving." I took Jase's hand and we walked out the door together.

"We can do this," he whispered in my ear.

I nodded. "I know we can." We hailed a cab to get to the train station. Jules and Aaron got in one behind us. "To the train station, please," I told the cab driver in Swiss. Aaron had taught me a few words so I could get around with little trouble. He nodded and began to drive away. We didn't get more than a block away when I heard a loud *boom* and our taxi began to swerve out of control. Then bullets began peppering the windshield. Our driver fell lifeless on the steering wheel. "Jase, get down!" I screamed as I went to grab the wheel.

He clutched my arm. "August, no! You'll be shot!"

I pulled myself free. "I'd rather be shot than crash!" Jase turned to look at the scene down the street. He gasped.

"The other taxi! They blew it up!" I looked behind us and saw the smoldering mess of Aaron and Jules' taxi.

"Oh my gosh…" I whispered.

"We have to go back!" he yelled.

"We can't," I answered through the tears streaming down my face. "We have to get to Japan and the safe house." I grabbed the wheel in an attempt to keep us on the road. A bullet then took out our front tire and the car started to swerve towards a building on the other side of the street. I jumped into the back seat and wrapped myself around Jase. He did the same to me. The car hit the building head on and jarred both of us. Luckily, I didn't feel too injured. "Let's get out of here!" I cried. I kicked the door open and saw that we were surrounded by men pointing machine guns at us. I noticed with dread that they were Hispanic. Santiago stepped out of the shadows.

"Hello, August," he greeted sinisterly. "Did you miss me?" He nodded to his men and they yanked me out of the car. I fell to the cobblestones with a cry. My face scraped against the rough stone and burned. One of the men pulled me roughly to my feet.

"Let her go!" Jase yelled. The men brought me to Santiago, who held up my chin so I was forced to look into his eyes.

"So this is the girl who wasn't supposed to exist," he mused. "Good thing I didn't kill you, *mi amor.* I will train you to be the best assassin in Europe. You can replace the one you killed in Germany!"

I pulled away from him. "Never!" I shouted. "I'd rather die."

Santiago laughed. "What about your boyfriend?" I watched in horror as the men pulled Jase out of the car and held a gun to his head.

"August, run!" he yelled. "Forget about me!"

"I'm not leaving you," I said with determination. "What do you want with me?" I asked.

"Don't listen to him!" Jase cried. "He'll kill you!"

He smirked. "I've seen the papers from the safe deposit box. I know your secrets, August. You will be the perfect addition to my team."

Jase was staring at our exchange in horror. "Let her go!" he cried. "I'm an inventor. I invented the Pegasus microchips and the Niebla drug. I'm worth more than her!"

Santiago smiled. "Bring them both," he ordered. The men began dragging both Jase and me towards an awaiting SUV. I tried to struggle, but they were too strong. Jase was yelling at Santiago and I was afraid that he would end up getting shot.

"Stay calm!" I shouted to him. "It'll be all right!" We were forced into the car. Santiago got in the front seat with another man.

"Go!" he commanded. The car took off.

I looked at Jase. "Niebla?" I asked. "Is that the drug that blocked my memory?"

"Yes," he answered sadly. "I wish I had never invented it. I never knew it would be used to hurt someone I love."

"The name sounds familiar," I stated.

"It's the Spanish word for 'fog.' We chose it because in most victims it makes them feel like they are in a fog for a while. I thought the effects would be temporary when I helped create it. I realized its power only when I saw it in practice. Most never regain their memories or go insane from trying to remember." He took my hands and stared into me with his deep brown eyes. "August, stop trying to remember. That drug will destroy your cognitive abilities if you keep attempting to recall that night. I won't let that happen to you."

I smiled. "Jase, my memories are the only thing left from the accident. I lost the papers with my parents' story. I have to regain my memories in order to know what happened. I won't stop."

"August, no. You'll go crazy."

"I haven't yet. I won't give up. If I go crazy, I go crazy. Forget about the drug. Right now we have to focus on escaping. Then we can figure out how to keep my head from exploding. Okay?"

"Fine," he replied. The men hadn't searched me for weapons, so I did have a knife in my boot. I sighed.

*I don't want to kill any more people. I can't. I have to do this delicately.*

156

I grabbed my knife and held it to the driver's throat. "Pull over!" I ordered in my most commanding voice. I glared at Santiago. "Tell him to pull over or I'll kill him," I said angrily.

The man glanced at me. "Go ahead. He's worthless to me. I'm in need of another driver anyway."

"August, don't," Jase pleaded. "He's innocent."

I thought about it for a moment, then I relaxed my grip and took it from the driver's neck. "He may be innocent, but Santiago isn't!" I went to stab him, but the car began to careen out of control. I screamed and fell into the back seat with Jase. Santiago was yelling commands at the driver in Spanish. I turned around and saw a silver car racing after our SUV. "Who is that?" I yelled to Jase over the commotion. "I swear if that's the CIA, I'll jump out of this car right now!"

"I don't know!" he answered. "But I'll jump with you!" I grabbed the door handle, but it was locked.

"Darn it!" I exclaimed. We were stuck. Both the CIA or Santiago would take us for our abilities and there was nothing I could do about it. *At least Aaron and Jules are dead and aren't suffering. They're safe. As long as they're safe, I'll go through whatever my enemies have planned for me.* I closed my eyes. *Maybe I'll die right here, in an accident like my parents. I'll see you soon, Mom and Dad.* Jase had his arms wrapped around me tightly and I knew he was preparing for the end. I grabbed his neck and kissed him with all the energy I could muster. For a moment, everything seemed to stop. We were just two teenagers kissing as if it was our last breath and we were going to spend it together.

"I love you," Jase whispered. I was about to reply when the car slammed into a building on my side. I felt something cut my right leg and I cried out in pain. "August!" he yelled.

"I'm okay," I replied. I saw Santiago was lying in the front seat in an unnatural position. "He's dead," I gasped. "Go. We've got to get out of here." Jase managed to get his door open and we started to run in the other direction in hopes the silver car wouldn't follow us. My leg was bleeding, but it wasn't fatal. I would survive. We ran until we heard a voice calling after us.

*"August! Jase!"* We stopped dead in our tracks and turned to see Aaron and Jules coming towards us.

"What?" I managed to say in shock. "You're alive?"

"What happened?" Jase asked with a stunned look on his face.

"They tried to kill us by bombing the car. Luckily, only the driver was killed," Aaron explained. "We stole a car and took off after you guys. Looks like we made it just in time. Come on, we have to get out of here before Celia shows up." I turned towards the car and went to follow Aaron. All of a sudden, I heard Jase cry out. I whipped around to see a wheezing Santiago holding a gun to Jase's head.

"No!" I shrieked. "Please, don't hurt him."

Santiago laughed. He was all bloody and awful looking. "Not so fast, August. I need to have a word with Aaron Steele." I saw Aaron reaching for his gun.

"Give me the boy, Santiago," he said carefully. "We can talk once he's free."

"I'll free the boy once you are dead," Santiago answered. "Don't make any sudden moves, Steele. I'll shoot this boy before you can draw your weapon."

"Go ahead," Aaron said. "Shoot me."

"Aaron, no," Jules pleaded.

"Aaron!" I cried.

Our enemy smirked. I wanted to smack it off his face. "Good choice, Steele. You knew you couldn't keep running forever." He took his gun from Jase's head and raised it towards Aaron. I gasped. I wasn't about to stand helplessly to the side while a man that I had grown to love died.

"Don't," Jase mouthed to me while shaking his head. He had realized what was going through my mind. I just gave a soft smile. As Santiago's finger went to the trigger, I raced in front of Aaron. There was the sound of a gunshot, then blistering, burning pain. I cried out as I collapsed to the ground. I heard another shot, but it didn't enter me. I closed my eyes to keep myself from realizing the pain I was in.

*"August!"* I heard Jase scream. I felt someone by my side shaking me. Jules was screaming at Aaron and blaming him.

*"You killed my cousin! You let her die!"* she shrieked angrily. *"You're a monster!"* I heard the sound of a slap and Aaron started yelling at her.

I didn't care anymore. *I'm dying. There's nothing anyone can do. At least the "final piece" is safe from Celia's grasp.*

*"August, baby, please wake up,"* Jase begged from far away. I felt him brush my hair from my face. I tried to stay awake, but I began to be pulled away.

*If this is death, then let it be.* There was a bright light and then everything faded to black.

# *15*

*Zurich, Switzerland*

Jase looked down at the lifeless body of August. She was bleeding heavily from a gunshot wound to her chest. "Why?" he asked in desperation.

Aaron stood from where he had been kneeling beside Santiago's body. He had shot him after August had taken the bullet meant for him. "She didn't want me to die," he answered. He got on his knees beside the blond girl and put two fingers to her neck. "She's alive," he said. "I can still feel a pulse." He took off his jacket and wrapped it around her wound to help stop the bleeding. Jules was standing off to the side with her hands over her mouth. She hadn't spoken a word since slapping Aaron across the face.

"She said that she wouldn't stop searching for the truth, even if it killed her," she put in softly. "We have to take her to the hospital."

"We can't," Aaron said firmly. "If we take her, then Celia will find us. We'll be sitting ducks."

"We can't just let her die!" Jase exclaimed.

"Sometimes you have to make sacrifices, Jase."

"Listen to you!" Jase screamed. "This is not some agent, Aaron! This is Conner's daughter!" He scooped up August's slim frame with ease. "I'm not about to let her die because of you. She's hurt because she thought your life was worth more than hers. I'm taking her to the hospital."

"If you go there, we're caught," Aaron warned.

"Too bad," Jules replied spitefully. "We're saving August." The two began to walk away. Aaron stayed where he was. He couldn't take that risk. Even though August had basically saved his life, he couldn't bring himself to go after them.

*I'll stay behind in case they need me. It won't do us any good to all be captured at the hospital. Jules and Jase can take care of her.* He sighed. The girl was starting to grow on him, no matter how annoying she was. "Be safe, kid," he whispered as he slipped down an alley.

~*O*~

The door to the trauma unit flew open as a team of doctors and nurses pushed a gurney down the hallway. The girl on the stretcher was bleeding from severe wounds to her leg and chest and none of the doctors' methods seemed to staunch them. She was unconscious and would certainly die if they couldn't stop the bleeding in time. "Prepare operating room three!" one nurse called.

Running behind the team were Jase and Jules. The woman was faster than the boy and had a determined look on her face. Jase was struggling to keep up. The doctors propelled the patient inside the operating room and the doors shut, which left the girl's two friends outside. They were gasping for air as they watched the scene from the doors. They had run to the hospital and now August had been swept away for surgery.

"Come on August, fight," Jules urged.

Jase was silent as he quietly encouraged his friend to wake

up. He stared desperately for any sign of life.

Inside the operating room, the physicians were struggling to stabilize the young girl. Her heart rate declined rapidly until it was a straight line. The heart monitor began to shriek in a warning. A defibrillator was quickly brought forward. One doctor grasped the paddles and quickly rubbed them together. "Clear!" he shouted before forcing them on the teenager's chest. Jules was sobbing on the other side of the door while Jase was trying to keep her steady. His eyes never wavered from the young woman.

Her heart still wasn't working. "Again!" the doctor yelled. "Clear!" August's slim body jumped from the gurney.

In the hallway, Jules was close to breaking down. Jase was the only thing keeping her from collapsing. An orderly came up to them and started speaking in Swiss. "I don't understand you!" Jules screamed angrily. "Speak English!"

"Jules, I think we should listen to him," Jase tried to say.

"Shut it, Jase!" The orderly pulled out a walkie-talkie and spoke rapidly into it. He gave them a smug look. "What did he say?" Jules asked.

"I don't know, but it must not be good," Jase replied. A security guard came running towards them.

"No, that's definitely not good," Jules agreed. The guard began to drag them away. "I'm not leaving," she said firmly. "My cousin is dying on the other side of that door. August!" she screamed. "August, fight! Don't let them win!" The guard continued down the hallway. "August!" she shrieked again. Jase kept his gaze on the door until it was out of sight.

*Don't let them win, sweetheart,* he begged internally. *You can beat this.* They were brought to a private waiting room.

"Stay here," the guard said with a heavy accent. They both nodded.

"Jules, we can't stay here forever," Jase said. "Aaron's right. Celia will come looking for us." The blond woman didn't answer. "Jules?" he asked softly.

She was crying, even though she was trying her best not to

show it. She sniffled and wiped her eyes with her sleeve. "I'm sorry," she apologized. "It's just, back there..." She broke down into sobs again. Jase quickly grabbed the box of tissues and handed them to her.

"It's okay," he soothed. "I know how you feel." He thought of the scene back in the operating room of his invincible girlfriend who was now so vulnerable and frail.

"I don't know what I'll do if she dies," Jules managed to choke. "I can't even imagine life without her."

"She is not going to die," Jase replied with determination. "August is strong. One bullet isn't enough to stop her."

"I'm going to kill Aaron," Jules said angrily. "He just left us without even thinking. I still have that engagement ring of his." She looked down at the diamond ring with fury. "Maybe I can sell it for some money to escape this nightmare."

"Aaron is used to being an independent spy," he explained. "He's not used to taking care of other people. August was dropped on him like a bomb. He had no idea what to do with a teenager. He wanted nothing to do with her, but took her in because Conner asked him to help her."

"How did they know one another?"

"They were business partners back in the nineties. Conner wasn't a spy, Jules. I know for a fact he wasn't. He was a civilian."

"Still, he shouldn't have left her. She saved his life."

"He'll come back," Jase replied. "Just give him some time to think." The door of the waiting room flew open and a woman they weren't expecting to see came strolling inside. She gave them both a calm smile.

"Hello," she greeted. "Can one of you tell me what's going on?"

~*O*~

I awoke in water. I was drowning and sloshing through it in a desperate attempt to swim. "Help!" I screamed. I slipped beneath the surface, but came up gasping for air.

*"Be strong, August. You still have a lot of strength left in you."* My father's last words rang through the water.

"Stop saying the same thing!" I yelled. "I'm trying! I'm trying to be strong, but I'm still stuck in this awful place! Why did you have to die?" I was being weighed down by my clothes. I kept screaming as I was drug beneath the surface. Instead of drowning, there was a bright light and the ocean faded away to a forest. I gasped. It was foggy and cold. I wrapped my arms around my chest to try to keep warm.

"Where am I?" I asked. I was on a trail, so I started to follow it. "Hello?" I called. There was a rustle in the nearby bushes. I began to run. The noise became louder as I fled through the forest. Suddenly, a house appeared in front of me and I smacked into the front door. I quickly threw it open and ran inside to a cozy looking living room.

My eyes grew wide. I knew this room. "I'm in my living room," I observed. I noticed that the pain in my leg and chest were completely gone. *Well that's not good.*

"August, wash up. Dinner will be ready soon." I looked up and saw my mother working away in the kitchen.

"Mom?" I asked in shock.

"Don't just stand there with your mouth open. Your dad will be home soon. Set the table, please."

I instinctively went to the cabinet to get the plates. Then I froze in my place. "You're dead," I said. "How am I talking to you?"

She gave me a soft smile. I then noticed how happy she seemed. There were no signs of worry around her eyes. She appeared to be twenty. Her blond hair was long and flowing again. "August honey, you know why you're here."

I realized the truth with horror. "I'm dead," I stated. "I died from that bullet, didn't I?"

My mother nodded. "I'm so sorry, baby." I ran to her and hugged her tightly.

"I can't be dead!" I shouted. "I have Jase! I have a life back there! I have to know your secrets!"

"You will. It was a mistake that landed you here. You were meant to survive that bullet. But I convinced Him to let me talk to you."

"Who's 'Him?'" I asked.

"You'll find out in due time," she replied mysteriously. "I can't tell you what our secrets are. But I know that you will figure them out. You have my smarts, August. You can find out the truth behind our deaths."

"I miss you so much, Mom," I managed to say.

She kissed my forehead. "I miss you too, sweetheart. We will see each other again. Not now, but later. You will discover our secrets one day. I know you can. Tell that boy of yours to take care of you. We might not be with you in the flesh, but we are always right here in your heart."

I hugged her even tighter. "Can you tell Dad something for me?"

"Of course."

"Tell him that I love him."

She smiled. "He already knows. I will tell him, though. Now it's time for you to go." A bright light began to fill the familiar living room. I clutched my mother as I felt her fading away. As the light overtook me, I heard one last phrase that I recognized from the accident.

*"Run as far and as fast as you can."*

I saw my lifeless body lying in a hospital bed in front of me. I smiled and ran towards her. *"I'm coming, Jase."*

~*O*~

Aaron watched the scene at the hospital. There were black SUV's and sedans everywhere. He saw Celia step from the lead car with Regan right behind her. *The others are going to be trapped. At least August might be dead. She won't have to suffer.* He still couldn't believe the teenager had taken a bullet for him. She was now dying in that hospital for him. *I can't believe I didn't go with them. What is the matter with me?*

He knew it was his training. He had been taught for so long to only care about himself. Everyone else was only a liability, even his partners. Conner was one and he was now dead. His other former partner Will was at a desk job since he didn't try to stop Aaron when he "went rogue." *He's lucky that he isn't dead.* Kara was alive only because she kept her connection to him a secret. He had gotten her a spot with the CIA, but that was all he did. After that, their meetings were clandestine. Now, his partner's daughter was lying in a hospital bed dying from a bullet meant for him.

*I have to go after her. If she dies, her blood is on my hands.* Aaron thought of Jules. *She's different from the other girls I've met. She's strong, courageous, and loyal. Not many people are like that these days. And I just let her go.*

*Get a grip,* another voice ordered. *You know the rule. Never fall in love. You know what happened to Rachel. The same thing could happen to Jules.*

*I know, but she's different. She knows that I'm a spy. Jules is strong enough to survive this world I live in. I can't believe I'm saying this…but I think I'm falling for her.*

All of a sudden, everything made sense. He was falling for Juliet Spencer. *I have to go back.* He put on his aviators and quietly made his way to the hospital. As he snuck in a back door, he smiled. *Who knew I could be won over by a civilian?*

I opened my eyes slowly. All I could see was white. *Did I die again?* My eyesight focused and I saw that I was in a hospital bed. There was a large bandage on my right thigh. I could feel more bandages wrapped tightly around my shoulder and chest. I could feel a dull ache through both wounds and it hurt to breathe. *I forgot about that.* The pain in my leg was worse because currently there was a certain nerdy boy lying across it asleep. "Jase!" I called hoarsely. He didn't move. "Jason!" I said a little louder as I tried to move my foot from underneath him. Finally, I snapped. "Jason Beckett, get off my leg before I cut off yours!"

He sat up with a start. "August?" he gasped.

"Hi," I greeted sheepishly.

"I was so worried," he said with concern. "We all thought you were…never mind."

"No, tell me," I demanded.

"August, your heart stopped twice on the operating table. We all thought you were going to die. But all of a sudden, your heart rate increased and the surgeons managed to patch up your injuries. You're expected to make a full recovery." I noticed that he had a strange look on his face.

"There's something else, isn't there?" I accused. I realized with terror that I was handcuffed to the bedframe.

He sighed. "Celia found us. She's getting ready to move us once you've recovered enough for transport."

I wanted to scream. *I'm not going back with that woman!* "Where's Jules?"

"She's already in custody. I arranged to stay with you until you woke up. I didn't want you to be alone."

I was touched. He was facing slavery, but still thought of me first. "Jase, I can't let you go with them. They'll keep you until they can squeeze all the worth out of you."

He smiled slightly. "I know. I'm not going to let them, though. I will fight for you, August. For us. We will be together someday. Who knows? Maybe you can be my handler or something."

"You know that will never happen," I said softly. "They want me to be some crazy assassin. They won't just stick me in any old job."

"Don't let them steal your humanity," he begged. "You're still innocent. They'll take that from you using every means they have. Remain my August." He leaned over and kissed me. Tears were streaming down my face as I returned the gesture. Jase wiped them away gently. "Don't let them see you broken," he whispered. "Fight them to your last breath. Stay strong and don't give up."

"I will," I replied with conviction. "Don't give up, either. I will find you if it takes me the rest of my life." Then the door opened and two men came in the room.

"Time to go," one said. Jase nodded, but didn't stand up. One of the men grabbed him and started to pull him from the room.

"I love you!" he yelled as he was dragged away. "Don't forget that!"

"*Jase!*" I screamed through my sobs. "I'll find you! I promise I'll find you!" I tried to stand to run after him, but the handcuff held me firm. The door was slammed shut and I fell back against my pillows in anguish. My body racked with sobs. *I'm stuck here. It's hopeless to escape. Jase is gone. Jules is gone. Aaron abandoned me. They will never let me go.*

The door opened once more and Celia strolled inside. She sat down on the chair beside my bed. "Hello, August," she said smugly.

"What do you want?" I asked with fury.

"I know that you have realized that you have no way to escape. I'm here to explain what will happen to you once we leave. Agent Regan is going to escort you to a private plane which will take you to Langley. From there, I'm going to have you sent to The Farm, our training facility. You'll be there at least two years. After that, I will place you in a position of my choice. You will have no say on the matter. If you're a good girl, I'll tell you your parents' secrets. Understand?"

I just nodded numbly. Celia smirked. She knew she had won. The elusive August Havens was in her grasp. She just had to pull the noose snug. "I saw your exchange with Jase. Maybe one day I'll allow you to call him." I watched as she walked into the hallway. *"Tell the men to add Beckett to the Lark subject list,"* I heard her say to Regan.

*Lark?* I vaguely remembered Celia asking if I had heard of an Operation Lark. *Why would she be adding Jase? This has got to be bad.*

A doctor came inside the room next.

"I'm here to give you something for the trip." He held up a syringe with a clear liquid inside. I gazed at him with dread.

"I'll go willingly," I bargained. "You don't need to drug me."

He looked at me with pity. "I'm sorry miss, but it's Director Keene's orders." He took my IV and slid the needle inside. I winced at the burning sensation from the medicine. I felt relaxed at once.

*Celia doesn't trust me. She knows that I'll try to escape.* I felt myself beginning to slip from reality.

*"Prepare her for transport,"* I heard Celia order faintly. *"We're leaving in ten minutes."*

Aaron snuck through the hallways of the hospital. He knew that Jules, Jase, and August were being held somewhere in the building. He just had to find them before Celia took them away. *Jase and August are top priority to the CIA. I'm probably only going to be able to save one of them. Jules is expendable. They won't worry about guarding her as much.* He looked in each room as he walked along. He was wearing doctor's scrubs, so he didn't seem suspicious. He wasn't sure how he was going to sneak his friends out under Celia's nose, but he was going to try anyway.

He was passing one room when a glimpse of blond hair caught his eye. Aaron stopped in his tracks and went up to the window in the door. There was a battered Juliet Spencer handcuffed to a table. She had more bruises on her face and arms. *She fought. She didn't give up easily.* Aaron was starting to have a growing respect for this woman. He opened the door and Jules looked up weakly. Her eyes grew wide when she saw him.

"Aaron?" she managed to say. "What are you doing here?"

"I'm coming to save you," he replied gently. "I'm sorry I left." He picked the lock on her handcuffs and helped her stand. She winced from the various bruises. "I'm sorry that happened to you again," he whispered. "I won't let them hurt you again."

She smiled. "Well this is a different side of you." She hissed as she began to walk. "That bullet is still killing me."

"I'll get you to a doctor once we're out of here. Where are Jase and August?"

"August is still in a hospital room down the hallway. They sedated her. I don't know where Jase is. I think he's already gone."

Aaron wanted to hit something. Because of his stupidity, Jase was back with the people who had tried to kill him before. August almost died because of her inability to back down from a fight. Jules was beaten because of her loyalty to her family. *I guess we all have our faults.* "Stand up straight," he ordered Jules. "You can't look injured. It will draw attention."

"I guess being beaten within an inch of my life isn't very inconspicuous, huh?" she joked.

"At least your sense of humor is intact," he replied with a grin.

She laughed. "It would be hard for them to take that away." They came up to a room that was being heavily guarded. Aaron stashed Jules in a storage closet and handed her a pistol.

"If anyone comes in here that even remotely looks like CIA, shoot them," he said firmly. She nodded and he went to free August. "I've been sent to escort Miss Havens to transport," he told the agents guarding her. "I have the papers verifying it here." He handed the lead agent a stack of papers that Kara had whipped up for him. The man looked them over and nodded. Aaron went inside the room and saw August lying unconscious in a bed. He grabbed the sides of the bed and began to push her from the room. "I have to administer some final tests to her before she can leave," he said to the agents firmly. "We have to make sure she's okay to be moved."

"We can do those tests in America," the lead agent replied gruffly.

"She could die if I don't complete them," Aaron disagreed. "Do you want to lose her?"

The three men looked at each other with just a hint of fear. They knew Celia would severely punish them if August died without becoming an agent. "Agent Duncan will accompany you to make sure Miss Havens is treated kindly," the lead agent answered. A young man with red hair and hazel eyes stepped forward. He already had his hand on his firearm.

*Well this will be easy.* "It won't take long," he said. "I only need to take some blood and an X-ray of her chest to make sure her ribs will heal properly." Agent Duncan nodded and followed him as he wheeled August towards the X-ray room. As they walked along, Aaron swiped a vial of adrenaline and a syringe from a medical table.

"What's that for?" Duncan asked suspiciously.

"It's for my next patient," he explained quickly. "He's having problems waking up." Duncan accepted the explanation and they entered the room. As soon as they were inside, Aaron grabbed the pressure point in the man's neck and he went down instantly. He swiped Duncan's pistol and prepared a syringe of the adrenaline. "I'm sorry, August," he said before slamming the needle into the young girl's heart.

# *16*

*Zurich, Switzerland*

I was wandering around in a dark fog when all of a sudden a burning sensation filled me. I gasped and felt myself floating rapidly out of the fog and back into reality. I sat up instantly and saw none other than Aaron Steele standing beside me. "Aaron?" I asked in shock as I fought to catch my breath.

"Yeah it's me, kid. Come on, Jules is waiting."

"What about Jase?"

He sighed. "Jase is gone, August. Celia already took him away. I'm sorry."

I shook my head. "No. I refuse to believe you. I'm going back for him." I got up to run after my boyfriend, but the handcuff held me back.

"August, please don't make me drug you. I don't want to, but I will to get you out of here alive. Just come with me. We'll go to a safe house and we'll figure out how to save Jase from there. Right now, we have to escape, though." He unlocked me from the handcuff.

I wanted to fight him, but I knew he was right. I had watched Jase be dragged away by agents. He was probably on his way to be forced into government slavery. *If I don't follow Aaron, I'll be in the same mess.* I followed Aaron from the room reluctantly and we crept towards a storage closet.

"I hid Jules in here," he explained. He handed me a gun and I took it. I kept an eye out for any agents while standing in the doorway. Jules and Aaron appeared from the shadowy room with no problems. Jules was also dressed in doctor's scrubs now. Aaron grabbed a gurney from the hallway. "Get on. We'll act like we're escorting you to transport, then slip away at the last second."

I nodded and lay down on the bed. Jules covered me with a sheet. "Stay still," she ordered. "Keep your eyes closed. You're supposed to be sedated." I obeyed and the two began to roll me down the hallway. I heard other men's voices soon enough.

"Where's Agent Duncan?"

"He stopped to get a cup of coffee. I brought along Heather for some backup to make sure Miss Havens reached her destination safely."

*Nice one, Aaron. Very smooth.*

"We'll take Miss Havens from here, doctor. You don't need to escort her."

*Oh, boy.* I slowly reached for the pistol hidden underneath the sheets.

"I'm afraid that isn't an option." I wrapped my hand around the grip and put a finger on the safety. All of a sudden, bullets began to fly. I opened my eyes, got my pistol, and started shooting.

"She's awake!" one agent yelled.

"Sorry to disappoint you, boys!" I shouted as I leaped from the bed and started to run. Jules and Aaron were right behind me.

"Why do you always have to be so cocky?" Jules asked as we reached the stairs.

"I think I get it from my dad," I replied. "Aaron, we can still get Jase."

"It's too late, August," he disagreed. "He's gone."

"I refuse to believe that." I turned to rush in the direction I had seen them take Jase. Aaron grabbed my shoulders and made me face him.

"They aren't going to hurt him," he explained forcefully. "He's too valuable. If they kill him, they'll lose one of the greatest inventors of the twenty first century. You however are only a teenage girl. They will most likely hurt you or capture you. You have to let him go."

I was crying at this point. "I can't. I can't leave him to be tortured by them."

"You have to." He took my hand and began to lead me away. Suddenly, we saw a mass of agents sprinting towards us. I knew what I had to do. I pushed Aaron and Jules into an elevator and pushed the up button. As we traveled upwards, I tried to think of how to say what I was planning.

"You have to go," I gasped.

"What?" Jules cried.

"I'm important to them. They won't kill me. I know they won't. You guys however are worthless. If you're caught, you're dead. I can lead them away."

"August, no," Aaron said. "We're staying together. I promised your father."

"I'm sorry," I replied. "But this will save you both." The elevator stopped and the door opened. I pushed the "3" button and the doors started to close.

"August, don't do this," Aaron pleaded.

"August!" Jules screamed right as the doors shut. I cocked my pistol and started to run. I found the stairwell leading to the roof and rushed up the stairs. As I sprinted, I heard ghostly voices in my head.

*"If they find out you exist, they will never let you go."*

*"You're the girl who wasn't supposed to exist."*

*"This is the story of two people who were never meant to fall in love."*

*"I'm going to keep you safe."*

*"Listen to me, sweetheart. This wasn't an accident, understand?"*

I reached the roof and pushed open the door. "I will remember," I said urgently. "Just not now." I stood on the ledge of the roof by another building. The stairwell entrance burst open and the agents came running out. I smiled cockily. "Hey, boys," I greeted. "Did you miss me?" They raised their guns to me. I closed my eyes and stepped off the narrow ledge. I heard the men yell as I jumped.

I landed on the roof below and sprinted towards the staircase. I pulled open the door and rushed down the stairs. I chose the closest room and got inside. I found myself standing inside a locker room. Without even thinking, I took a weight and used it to break one of the flimsy locks. I pulled off the hospital gown and dressed in a pair of jeans, a black t-shirt, and a denim jacket. I put my hair back in a high ponytail, threw my clothes in the locker, and hurried out the back door into the gym.

As soon as I ran out, I smacked into someone I wasn't too happy to see. He smirked at me. "Hi, August." It was Agent Regan. "Let's go." He went to lead me away. Unfortunately, I wasn't going down without a fight. I kicked him in the shin and ran for my life. I kept a firm hand on my pistol. I wasn't going to use it unless I absolutely had to. *"She's heading towards the front doors,"* I heard Regan say. *"Lock down the gym."*

*I can't kill another person. I just can't.* A shot rang out and I plastered myself to the floor. I began to crawl towards the exit. People were screaming and running in the same direction. I stood up and another bullet barely missed me. My chest burned from the effort of trying to move. *There's no other way. If you want to survive, you know what you have to do.*

I sighed and turned around. Regan pointed his gun at me. "Don't move," he ordered.

I was crying and gasping for air. "I'm sorry," I choked. "But I'm not going to jail." His finger went to the trigger. Without even thinking, I pulled out my gun and shot him before sprinting away from the scene. I saw him collapse to the floor. *What have I done?* As I rushed out of the gym, I spotted a payphone. There was some change in my pocket, so I dialed Kara's number.

*"Who is this?"*

"It's August. I don't have much time. I need help." I could hear sirens screaming in the distance.

*"Of course. Where are you?"*

"I'm in Zurich."

*"All right. I'm going to send a new identity to one of my contacts there. He'll take it to the airport. He'll find you. You have tickets on a flight to Lisbon in an hour. Hurry."* She hung up and I went to hail a cab to take me to the airport.

As I traveled, I leaned back in my seat and tried not to think about the person I had most likely killed. *He was going to take me to jail. I couldn't just go with him.* The cab pulled up to the airport and I paid him using money I'd found in a wallet in the locker room. I ran inside the terminal and waited to be found by Kara's contact. A man bumped into me almost immediately and pressed a piece of paper in my hand. There was nothing on it except the number 457 and a key wrapped inside. I found the lockers and opened number 457 with the key. Inside the small box were a passport, a driver's license, and tickets for a flight to Lisbon all with the name "Charlotte Geist" on them. There was also a paper with my backstory typed on it. I grabbed all the papers and hurried to security.

Security was a breeze and I made it to my plane in time. As it ascended, I finally breathed a sigh of relief. *I made it.*

~*O*~

I was sitting in Kara's apartment again as she did my hair. It was now a startling red color and my eyes were hazel. My name was still Charlotte Geist. "Where do you want to go?" Kara asked. "I could send you to one of Aaron's safe houses in Asia."

"No, not there," I disagreed. "I want to find Jase. I just let him get captured."

"I don't know where he is, August. He just vanished. None of my contacts have information about him."

"They'll take him to America," I said. "I know they will."

"How can you possibly know that? The CIA will hide him away."

"Celia will want me to find him. She'll put him in plain sight."

"You can't be certain."

"No, I can't," I answered with a smile. "But I can try to find him. Plus I can keep an eye on Natalie and Blaire. Celia will probably target them for leverage."

Kara shook her head. "You're insane."

"I am my father's daughter," I replied.

"Fine. I'll help you. But just so know, Aaron will not set foot on American soil again. Celia will have him killed as soon as he does. You'll be on your own. No extractions or assistance."

"I can live with that," I said. "Just give me some weapons."

"First, I'll have to set up a safe house in Philadelphia. I'll send some of my trusted contacts over there to design one. You'll have to stay here a few days. It will give you some time to relax while the heat dies down. The agent you shot is in critical condition."

I nodded. I didn't like the idea of just sitting around while Jase was forced to work as a slave to the government, but it was my only option. *I will find you, Jason Beckett. Not today, but someday.*

~*O*~

Celia Keene stalked into the Zurich field office. *"Where is she?"* she yelled at her team.

"She escaped custody, ma'am," one agent replied meekly.

"She was sedated!" Celia screamed. "How could she possibly escape?" She angrily threw a stack of papers off a desk. "August Havens is our top priority, people! If we lose her, we lose *everything!*"

"Aaron Steele and Juliet Spencer helped her," another female agent explained. "I have security footage of them freeing her. It seems that Steele gave her a shot of adrenaline to wake her up. From there, he and Miss Spencer made her appear still sedated and planned on rolling her out of the hospital. Our agents tried to stop them, but they separated and got out of the building. August actually jumped off the roof to the adjoining building."

"Yes, where she shot Agent Regan," one agent spoke up.

"Agent Regan is dead," Celia replied tiredly. "He died from his injuries one hour ago." The other agents began talking among each other in horror. "Operation Lark is still in effect," she proclaimed loudly. "August can't hide forever. If she's separated from Steele, she's vulnerable. She'll go after her precious Jason. We can catch her and we will. We can use this to our advantage." She smirked evilly. "Run as fast as you can, August, but we will find you."

~*O*~

Aaron and Jules were driving through Europe together. Jules had been awkwardly silent during the entire ride and he could almost feel the hatred coming from her. "I'm sorry," he said. "But I had to drug you."

"You could have gone back for her. We could have forced her to come with us," Jules replied with contempt.

"It was too late. She made her choice, which was to stay behind and lead the agents away from us."

"She killed another person, Aaron."

"August could have handled it a different way. But Regan wasn't about to give up. She shot him to save herself from being taken away."

"I just can't imagine her as a murderer."

"Don't. She is still the August you know. She just had to change in order to survive. Don't blame her for what she has done. If anything, blame me. I dragged her into this world."

She gave a small smile. "It wasn't your fault, either. You saved her from those people. Now she's making her own way. Kara told us she was looking for Jase."

"August shouldn't have to be alone," Aaron said angrily. "She did make her choice, but we could have made it out alive. I could have found Jase with her."

"Well, she's stubborn," Jules replied. "She's a lot like her mother in that regard."

"I guess," Aaron sighed.

"So where are we going?" she asked with a grin.

"Wherever you want to go," he answered. "You can decide."

She thought for a moment. "Paris," she finally chose. "I've always wanted to go there."

He nodded. "Then Paris it will be. I already have a safe house there."

"Aaron, why did you choose to save me? You could have gone after Jase." She looked at him strangely. "Do you like me?"

He had just the hint of a smile on his lips. "Yes, Jules," he said. "I do."

"Good," she replied. "I like you, too." She leaned over and kissed him softly on the lips. He returned the gesture with fiery passion. At that moment, neither of them cared about August and Jase being alone. It was just them together sharing a moment that was intimate and pure. All of the other dangers could come later. As long as they were together, they could conquer whatever the CIA threw their way.

~*O*~

Jase looked up from the floor of the SUV. He had been traveling for the past few days and was ready to be in an actual bed. The handcuffs chafed against his sore wrists and he winced. He thought of the girl he had left behind in a hospital in Zurich. "August..." he whispered. "I'm sorry."

"Still mumbling about your girlfriend, Beckett?" the agent escorting him asked gruffly.

"No," he lied.

"You know you'll never see her again, right?"

Jase smiled. "You don't know her like I do." He slowly reached in his pocket.

"What do you mean?"

Jase pulled out his phone and looked at his background of August, Aaron, and him at Checkpoint Charlie. The agents who had captured him had been foolish enough to believe he couldn't do anything with the phone since it had no service. Unfortunately for them, he was smart enough to find loopholes around that problem. He began to quietly type an email. "August never gives up. Celia will have to eliminate her before she'll stop looking for me." He finished typing and hit "send." The driver didn't even notice.

"It sounds like she'll be an interesting chase."

He grinned. "You have no idea."

~*O*~

I hoisted my suitcase over the door frame and walked into my new apartment building. I brushed my red hair from my eyes and went to get my key from the front desk. "Here you go, Miss Geist," the friendly landlady said while handing it to me. "Enjoy your new home."

"Thank you," I replied. "I will." I went to the elevator and pushed the "5" button. I had not been inside my apartment yet, but Kara had put everything together for me. I trusted her. As the elevator ascended, all I could think of was how I could possibly be alive. Over the past two weeks, I had been kidnapped, tortured, beaten, arrested, drowned, shot, and even died. Somehow I had managed to survive. *I'm tougher than I look,* I thought with amusement.

The elevator stopped at my floor and I pulled my suitcase down towards my door. I had been staying with Kara for the past four days and she had made sure I only had to bring my clothes and meager possessions with me. I had planned on sneaking into our home and stealing family photos later once the CIA had finished cataloging everything we owned. I couldn't believe I had to resort to stealing my own possessions.

*Mom, Dad, I will find out whatever you've hidden from me.* Kara had not allowed me to take the box with me since she had already shipped it to Aaron's new safe house. She asked me repeatedly if I wanted to join them, but I declined. I had to stay behind and find Jase. However, I had set up a box at the post office so they could send me letters. Once I found Jase's location, I would find a way to make contact with him. Then we could join Aaron and Jules and create a new life.

I opened my door and walked into my new home. It was small, but nicely decorated. There was a combined kitchen and living room, a bathroom, a bedroom, and another room set up as an office. I put my suitcase in my bedroom and sat down on the comfy tan couch with a sigh. My phone beeped suddenly. I picked it up and saw I had a new email. I had to laugh when I saw the subject line.

"Catch me if you can," I read. "Oh, Jase." I blew out a breath and smiled. *Try finding me now, Celia. I'll be right in plain sight. And I will find you, Jase. Don't give up. I'm coming for you.*

My name is August Havens. I'm the girl who wasn't supposed to exist, but has survived against all odds. Nothing will stop me from finding the truth about my parents. You'll have to kill me before I'll stop searching.


To be continued…

# ACKNOWLEDGMENTS

Okay, first let me thank you, reader, for reaching the end of the book. I wouldn't be here if it wasn't for you. I hope you enjoyed it and had fun with August along the way. She's a fun character, right? Stick around for the rest of the series!

Writing *Wanted* was an incredible experience. I got to create a new world using my imagination and I loved it. I've been working on this story for the past three years and now I believe it's ready to share with the world. I hope it is an enjoyable story and you readers fall in love with it just like others have. Here's some people that I have to thank because if they hadn't supported me, this story never would have seen the light of day.

To Mom and Dad, thanks for putting up with me becoming a writer. I know it was hard sometimes when I didn't do what I was supposed to and it seemed impossible, but at least you allowed me to keep writing. I did end up pulling a 3.86 GPA, though! Thanks to Dad for introducing me to action movies, too! *Wanted* wouldn't be here if you hadn't! Also, thanks for being a great guinea pig reader and helping me make this book more realistic when it comes to the action scenes. Mom, thanks for being supportive and coming up with ideas with me along with helping me format. I love you!

Thanks to Katelyn, Lindsay, and Sam for being the best friends ever and putting up with my craziness! I absolutely love the cover and Katelyn did such a great job! You are now my official cover artist! (You were a gorgeous model too, Lindsay. You really brought August to life.) Sam, thanks for always being there and encouraging me to make my dream a reality! I love all three of you and you are the best sisters I could ever ask for!

Ellie and Bekah, I didn't forget you either! You guys are the best and thanks for being my PR people and spreading the word about my book! You're the most awesome guinea pig readers! I love spending time with you guys at school!

Thanks to Mrs. Sally Jo Herring for inspiring me to become an author and being willing to read the first (awful) draft of *Wanted* all the way back in my senior year of high school. I still use your grammar tricks to this day. I miss you and your red pen!

Cristi, you're awesome (just saying.) You're a mother of three and you took time out of your busy schedule to read your cousin's book and edit it! This book wouldn't be as good as it is if you hadn't worked on it! (I'll get royalty money to you eventually.)

Tiffani, thanks for being my NaNoWriMo buddy! I loved our writing times together after choir! Get your book to me sometime! I'm excited to read it!

Thanks to the people from high school for supporting me even when I was an ordinary girl with an impossible dream. Hopefully this will be something to talk about at our reunion!

And to all the people who first read *Wanted* back when it was poorly written and thought it was amazing, thanks so much for your constant support and encouragement. I wouldn't be the writer I am today if it wasn't for you guys. You're the reason why *Wanted* exists. I hope to see you all around!

And to God be the glory. He gave me these abilities and I am only able to publish this book because of Him. I hope and pray that He allows me to keep developing my writing and

growing in my faith.
Thank you for reading *Wanted.*

# ABOUT THE AUTHOR

Shelby Haisley is studying to be a clinical therapist. She has enjoyed psychological thrillers and espionage stories, such as the *Bourne* series and *Mission: Impossible*, and wanted to write one of her own. *Wanted* was inspired by watching these movies. She decided it was time for a female heroine to step into the action scene, thus August Havens was born and her story began. Shelby lives in Indiana with two cats and two German Shepherds.

Made in the USA
Charleston, SC
02 February 2014